"You leave me no choice, Princess."

Then he tipped her chin up and leaned forward. Anticipation pulsed through her veins. Every single second was an unnerving kind of torture. And finally, his mouth was on hers, his hand coming to wrap more firmly around her jaw, as if he couldn't get enough, as if he would devour her.

Long live the king!

She touched his face, and a groan erupted from his throat.

A whimpering, mewling sound came from hers. Mortification would have set in, if the king wasn't equally as needy.

After who knew how long, Juan Carlos placed his hands on both her shoulders and, she sensed, with great reluctance eased her away.

He leaned back against the seat, breathing hard. "I've never made love to a woman in a limo before, Princess. But it wouldn't take much to change that."

* * *

A Royal Temptation is part of the series Dynasties: The Montoros—One royal family must choose between love and destiny!

A ROYAL TEMPTATION

BY
CHARLENE SANDS

MILLS & BOON

First published in Great Britain 2015
by Mills & Boon, an imprint of Harlequin (UK) Limited,
Eton House, 18-24 Paradise Road, Richmond, Surrey, TW9 1SR

© 2015 Harlequin Books S.A.

Special thanks and acknowledgment are given to Charlene Sands
for her contribution to the *Dynasties: The Montoros* miniseries.

ISBN: 978-0-263-25907-0

Harlequin (UK) Limited's policy is to use papers that are natural,
renewable and recyclable products and made from wood grown in
sustainable forests. The logging and manufacturing processes conform
to the legal environmental regulations of the country of origin.

Printed and bound in Great Britain
by CPI Antony Rowe, Chippenham, Wiltshire

Charlene Sands is a *USA TODAY* bestselling author of more than thirty-five romance novels, writing sensual contemporary romances and stories of the Old West. Her books have been honored with a National Readers' Choice Award, a CataRomance Reviewers' Choice Award, and she's a double recipient of the Booksellers' Best Award. She belongs to the Orange County chapter and the Los Angeles chapter of RWA.

Charlene writes "hunky heroes with heart." She knows a little something about true romance—she married her high school sweetheart! When not writing, Charlene enjoys sunny Pacific beaches, great coffee, reading books from her favourite authors and spending time with her family. You can find her on Facebook and Twitter. Charlene loves to hear from her readers! You can write her at PO Box 4883, West Hills, CA 91308, USA or sign up for her newsletter for fun blogs and ongoing contests at charlenesands.com.

To Allyson Pearlman, Robin Rose,
Mary Hernandez and Pam Frendian. You're my crew,
my Best Friends Forever. Your friendship puts
lightness in my heart and a smile on my face every
day. I am surrounded by the best and I love you dearly.

One

Juan Carlos Salazar II stood at the altar in Saint Lucia's Cathedral, holding his head high as he accepted the responsibility and honor of being crowned King Montoro of Alma. In a dreamlike state he went through the motions that would bring the monarchy back to what it had once been decades ago. He'd been orphaned at a young age and taken in by his uncle. Since then, he'd lived a life filled with determination and dignity. He'd always known great things would come to him if he worked hard and kept his focus. But king? Never in his life would he have guessed his own true destiny.

With the golden orb and blessed scepter in his hands, he saw the austere ceremony in the cathedral was coming to a close. Prime Minister Rivera had given a speech full of renewed hope for the country, the small set of islands off the coast of Spain that had been ravaged by the now overthrown dictatorship of the Tantaberras. Seventy years of oppression overturned by loyal citizens, who looked to Juan Carlos for the reinstatement of a monarchy that would capture their hearts and minds.

Archbishop Santiago placed the royal robe over Juan Carlos's shoulders. As he took his seat on the throne, the archbishop set the jeweled crown of Alma upon his head. All of the tradition, ritual and protocol of the coronation had been observed, and he was now King Montoro of

Alma, the true heir to the throne. He spoke an oath and vowed to be much more than a figurehead as he promised to restore order and hope to the country.

It was a monumental time in Alma's history and he was happy to have the support of his cousins, Gabriel, Rafe and Bella. They were smiling and nodding their approval from their seats, Bella with tears in her eyes. They'd all lived and thrived in the United States before this, and forgive him, but heaven knew Rafe and Gabriel, who were once thought to be first in line to the throne but had been disqualified for separate and unique reasons, were not cut out for the rigors and sacrifice of royal life. They were only too glad to see Juan Carlos accept the position of sovereign.

A woman seated several rows behind his cousins caught his attention. Deep cerulean-blue eyes, clear and large, stood out against her porcelain face and white-blond hair. She reminded him of a snow queen from a fairy tale in his youth. And as he was ushered down the aisle after the coronation their gazes locked for an instant and her one eyelid closed in a wink. Was it for him? His lips immediately quirked up at the notion and he forced the smile from his expression. Still, his heart did a little tumble as it had been doing all day, but this time it was the woman, and not the ceremony, that had caused the commotion.

The next hour passed, again in dreamlike wonder, as he was escorted out of the cathedral by Alma's finest royal guards, to be met with unrestrained jubilation all along the parade route. He sat atop a convertible car and waved with gloved hands, as they made their way toward the palace. And there, on the top steps of Alma's regal old-world palace, Juan Carlos began his first speech as king.

"Citizens of Alma, as your new king, I promise to honor the sovereignty of our nation, to always put the country first and to work alongside our parliament to restore our democracy. It is a vow I take with an open but steady heart and a determination to see that our freedoms are never threatened again."

Cheers went up. "Viva Juan Carlos!"

Juan Carlos waited until the crowd calmed to finish a speech that was interrupted three more times by applause.

He left the palace steps energized, instilled with the very same hope he saw in the eyes of his fellow countrymen. He was a foreigner, by all rights, an American, and yet, they'd accepted him and looked to him to help establish a newer, brighter Alma.

He would not let them down.

As austere as his day was, he took a moment to reflect on the coronation and picture the beautiful woman in the light blue chiffon gown, her eyes as vibrant as deep ocean waters. He'd searched for her during the procession, the parade and the speech that followed, only to be disappointed.

She'd been a diversion from the gravity of the day.

Winking at him had brought a smile to his lips.

Who was she?

And would she have his children?

"Do I need to call you Your Highness?" his cousin Rafe asked as he pumped Juan Carlos's hand. They stood off to the side in the palace's grand ballroom. The coronation gala was well underway and the orchestra played lively tunes. An array of fresh flowers decorated the arched entryways, aisles and tables.

"You mean, as opposed to Squirt, Idiot and Bonehead like when we were kids?"

"Hey, I wasn't that bad."

"You were a year older and that gave you bullying rights."

"Okay, guilty as charged. But now you can have me hung by the neck until dead."

"I could've done that to you back then, too."

"Ha, funny."

"Call me Juan Carlos or cuz, just like you do now. Your Highness comes into play only on formal occasions or royal business."

All amusement on his cousin's face disappeared. "Seriously, Juan Carlos, congratulations. The family is proud of you. You're the only one of the lot who was cut out for this. You are honoring our aunt Isabella's final wishes by restoring the monarchy."

Juan Carlos came to the throne quite by accident, after Bella discovered a secret cache of letters that revealed Rafe, Gabriel and Bella's late grandfather, Raphael Montoro II, was illegitimate and not the true heir to the throne. As such, neither of Juan Carlos's cousins would have been the rightful king. The former queen's indiscretion had been kept hidden all these years until her great-grandchildren had uncovered it.

"Thank you, cousin. I've thought about my grandmother these past few weeks and I think she would approve. It means a great deal to me." He sighed. "I hope to make a diff—" He caught a glimpse of a woman in blue and craned his neck to get a better look.

It was her. She was attending the gala. Only dignitaries, friends and family members along with the royal photographers and journalists had been invited to the party, two hundred strong.

"Hey," Rafe asked. "What are you stretching your neck to see?"

"She's here," he muttered, without shifting his gaze. She was standing near an archway leading to the foyer, looking to make an escape.

"Juan Carlos?"

"Oh, uh, I saw a woman at the coronation and I haven't stopped thinking about her."

"This I've got to see. Any woman who can take your

mind off a day as big as this has got to be something special. Where is she?"

"I'm not going to point. Just look for the most beautiful woman in the room and you'll find her."

"Emily is right there, talking to Bella."

"Spoken like a besotted newlywed. Okay, yes, Emily is gorgeous, now find a woman in blue who is not your wife."

"If you'd agreed to a formal receiving line, you'd have met her already."

He hadn't wanted a stiff, awkward line of people congratulating him. He'd make his way over to his guests and speak with them during the course of the evening. He'd vowed to be a king *of* the people and *for* the people and that started right now. "Do you see her?"

"Ah, I do see her now. Very blonde, nice body, great eyes."

"That's her. Do you know who she is?"

"No, but apparently she knows Alex and Maria Ramon. They just walked up to her and they appear friendly."

"Well, then, I think it's time I spoke with Alma's deputy prime minister of commerce and his wife, don't you?"

Juan Carlos moved swiftly across the ballroom and as he approached, Alex spotted him and smiled. "Your Highness." Juan Carlos nodded. It would take some time getting used to that greeting.

Maria, not one to stand on ceremony, hugged his neck. She and Alex had just married and postponed their honeymoon to attend the coronation. "I'm happy to see this day, Your Highness. You are just what Alma needs."

"Thank you, Maria."

As he made eye contact with the blonde woman, it felt as if something quick and sharp had pierced his body. Her eyes were large, shaped like perfect twin almonds, the sparkle in them as bright as any star. Mesmerized, he couldn't look away.

"And please, let me introduce you to Portia Lindstrom, Princess of Samforstand."

Princess?

She *could* have his children.

Juan Carlos offered her his hand and at the touch of her delicate palm, he once again felt that quick, sharp sensation. "Nice to meet you, Princess. I'm glad you could make the coronation. It's a good day for Alma, I hope."

"I'm sure it will be, Your Majesty. And please, call me Portia."

"I will," he said. "If you call me Juan Carlos."

A pink cast tinged her porcelain skin. "I couldn't."

"Why not?"

"Because, you're the king."

"I'll let you in on a secret. Up until a few months ago, I was living in Miami and running a rather large business conglomerate. I'm afraid I still have American ties and king is not in their vocabulary, unless we're talking about Elvis."

She smiled. "I live in America, too. I'm on the west coast right now. My family was from a tiny country near Scandinavia."

"Well, then, we have a lot in common. As you can see, Alma is not a large country, either."

Maria and Alex exchanged looks and excused themselves. He'd forgotten they were there. It was rude of him. But now, he was alone with Portia.

"You are a curiosity. You won't call me Juan Carlos, but yet you wink at me just as I am crowned king."

Portia froze. Surely the king didn't believe she'd actually winked at him. It was that darn nervous twitch of hers. It would have to happen at the exact moment she'd first made eye contact with him. She should be immune to royalty—she'd met enough princes and princesses in her twenty-eight years—but Juan Carlos Salazar seemed different, strikingly handsome and down to earth. Before she could explain about the wink, the orchestra began playing a lovely Latin waltz.

He bowed in old world fashion. "Princess Portia, I'd be honored if you danced with me."

"I'm afraid I don't waltz."

"Neither do I," he replied. "We can wing it and set a new trend."

She chuckled. He didn't act like the stuffed-shirt royals she'd met in the past, and when he took her hand and led her to the unoccupied dance floor, she didn't protest. He was a better dancer than he let on, and she glided across the floor with him, fully aware every set of eyes in the room were on them.

"We're the only ones out here," she whispered.

He grinned, flashing white teeth against golden-brown skin. He was tall and dashing and at the moment, charming her silly by staring into her eyes as if she was the only person who existed in the world. It was quite flattering.

"Don't worry. Other guests will join in after the king's first dance. It's tradition."

"Then I should be honored you picked me."

"After that wink, how could I not pick you?" He held her possessively and spoke with authority, as if he'd been king all of his life.

"It was a twitch. I had something in my eye."

"I choose to believe it was a wink."

"Yes, Your Highness."

He smiled again and moved her across the dance floor as if she were light as air.

When the dance ended, he didn't release her hand. "Will you take a walk with me?"

"You want to leave your own gala?"

He shrugged and didn't appear worried. "It's been a long, monumental day. I could use a little break."

Portia couldn't very well say no. And getting some fresh air did sound good. Because of her title, she'd been invited to the gala, and to refuse such a high honor would've been unheard of. Her mother and father's greatest wish, as her grandmother told it, was for her to remain true to her royal bloodlines, even while having a career and life of her own. So she juggled her time accordingly, to honor her deceased parents' wishes. She hadn't had enough time with them, but she'd hoped to make them proud. "Well, then, yes. I'll walk with you."

They strode off the dance floor in silence. His hand pressed to her back, he guided her toward a small back door and they ducked out to a deserted foyer. "There are private gardens just outside where we can sit."

He opened a door she was sure only royals were privy to, and a gust of cool autumn air hit her. Without a second's hesitation, Juan Carlos removed his tuxedo jacket and placed it around her shoulders. "Better?"

"Yes, thank you." She tugged the lapels closed and kept her hands there, away from the king's tempting grasp. His dark eyes were on her every move, and when he touched her, her pulse raced in a way it hadn't in a very long time.

He led her to grounds surrounded by lattices covered with vines. "Would you like to sit down?"

"Okay."

She sat on a delicately woven rattan love seat and he lowered down beside her, his six-foot presence looming large next to her. Aware of the solid breadth of his shoulders and the scent of his skin, she found the new king of Alma a little too appealing. "It's nice here. Quiet," she said. "You must be exhausted."

"Yes, but invigorated, too. If that makes any sense to you."

"It does. When I'm researching a piece of art for a client, I might work sixteen-hour days, but I always get excited when I locate it." His brows came together as if he were puzzled. "I'm an art advisor," she explained. "I help collectors build their collections."

"Impressive. And do you work in your country?"

"I'm based out of Los Angeles and New York. I don't spend any time in Samforstand."

"That's how it was for me. I worked out of Miami and New York, but now, Alma will be my permanent home. My duty is here and I will adjust. The country is beautiful, so it won't be a hardship."

"Excuse me, Your Highness," said a voice from behind the bench.

"Yes?" Juan Carlos turned around.

"I'm sorry to interrupt, but Chancellor Benoit has been called away and insists on saying his farewells to you personally. He is waiting in the antechamber."

"All right, thank you. Please tell the chancellor I will be in to see him shortly."

The man gave a curt nod and walked off.

"Well, looks like duty calls. I'm sorry." He rose and extended his hand. "Please save another dance for me tonight, Portia. There's more I want to learn about...*art advising*." He smiled.

Her heart hammered. She didn't know what to make of the cocoon-like hold he had on her. She'd only just met him and already he was wrapping himself around her thoughts with his silent compliments and easy ways. "I will."

She rose and he walked her back to the ballroom, depositing her exactly where he'd found her, beside Maria and Alex.

"I will be back," he said.

Portia's throat hitched and she nodded.

"Looks like the king is smitten." Maria kept her voice

low enough for only Portia's ears. She was sure Maria, a public relations expert and friend, had been instrumental in her receiving an invitation to the coronation and gala.

"He's being gracious, Maria."

Maria seemed to ignore her comment. "He's a good man."

"Perfect for Alma. But not for me." She was attracted to Juan Carlos. Any woman with blood running through her veins would be, but talk about high profile. You couldn't get much higher, and that's the last thing Portia needed in her life. It had taken her three years to climb out of the hole she'd dug for herself by getting involved with the Duke of Discourse, Travis Miles, LA's favorite talk show host.

Charming, debonair and controversial, he'd dragged her into his limelight from the start of their love affair to the bitter, heartbreaking end. Her career had suffered as the details of his neglect and wandering eye came into play. She'd almost lost all credibility with her clients. Luckily, she'd managed her way out of that situation, vowing to keep a low profile, stay in the small circle of the art world and not allow another high-profile charmer to get to her. And that included the king of Alma.

"I don't know about that," Maria said, matter-of-factly.

"I do," she said, convincing herself of that very thing. "I have an important meeting in Los Angeles with a client in a few days."

"A lot could happen in a few days, Portia."

But the conversation ended when a nice-looking gentleman approached, introduced himself as Alma's secretary of defense, and asked her to dance.

Portia accepted, and as she was being led to the dance floor, shot an over-the-shoulder glance at Maria.

Only to find Juan Carlos standing there, his gaze following her every movement.

He had indeed come back for her.

* * *

Gnashing his teeth, Juan Carlos ran a hand down his face to cover the tightness in his jaw. Princess Portia had danced nonstop with three men since he'd returned from seeing Chancellor Benoit off. Every time Juan Carlos thought to approach, he was interrupted or summoned into a conversation with a group of dignitaries. He couldn't fall short of his duties on his coronation day, yet the beautiful snow queen consumed his thoughts, and as he spoke with others, he kept one eye on Portia.

Finally free from conversations, he had an aide approach the orchestra and suggest that they take a five-minute break. The music died instantly and Juan Carlos strode over to the table where Portia had just taken a seat. "Hello again."

Those startling blue eyes lifted to him. "Hello."

"I'm happy to see you having a good time."

"I am," she said. "Would you like to sit down?"

"I have a better idea."

Her eyes twinkled. "Really? What would that be?"

He offered his hand again, hoping she'd take it. "Come with me and find out."

Her hesitation rattled his nerves. "Where?"

"Trust me and I'll show you."

She rose then, and as they walked out of the ballroom again with her hand in his, she watched him carefully. She had no reason not to trust him. He would never steer her wrong.

"In here," he said.

He tugged her into a spacious office and shut the door. It was black as coal at first, but the light of the full moon streamed in and his eyes adjusted so that he could make out Portia's silhouette. He took her gently into his arms and overwhelming sensations rushed through his body. Silently, with a look, she questioned his actions, but with his eyes he assured her she had nothing to fear. Then the orchestra began playing and as music piped into the room through the air ducts, he began to move her along to the beat. She tossed her head back and laughed. "You aren't serious."

He grinned. "It's the only way I can assure us not being interrupted again."

"You are resourceful, Your Highness. We have an entire dance floor all to ourselves."

"What would make it perfect would be if you'd call me Juan Carlos."

"But you've earned the right to be called king."

"Tonight, for now, think of me as a man, and not a king."

"I'll try, but you have to understand, after all the adoration, the photos and parades and galas in your honor, it's not easy for me."

He did understand, but pressed his reasoning a little further. "Think of it this way. How would you like it if everyone you knew called you Princess Portia?"

She gave it some thought and nodded. "I see your point."

He drew her inches closer, so that her sweet breaths touched his face, but he didn't dare do more. Though he wanted to crush her against him, feel her body sway with his, he couldn't rush her or scare her off. These feelings pulsed through him with near desperation. He'd never been so…besotted. Such an old-world word, but that's exactly how he felt.

"How long will you be in Alma?" he asked.

"I leave for the States in two days. I'm due back at work."

News he didn't want to hear. "Are you working with a client?"

"Yes, he's someone very influential and I'm thrilled to have the chance to meet with him for the first time. He's new to collecting, and I have an interview with him to see where his tastes lie."

"I see. It's a good opportunity for you. I would imagine being Princess Portia of Samforstand carries some weight in your line of work."

"I'll admit, using my royal heritage has helped me attain clients, but it's my expertise that has earned their trust."

"Trust is important," he said.

"You have the trust of the entire country right now."

"Yes," he said, sighing. "It's a big responsibility. I'm sure you take your responsibility seriously."

"I do. My reputation earns me that trust and I guard it like a mother would her child."

He smiled at the image gathering in his mind, of Portia, mother of his child.

Dios. He was in deep. How was it possible? He had known her less than a day.

And already, he was naming their first-born child.

Two

Stately and grand, Portia's hotel in Del Sol was just a short distance from the palace. The big bed in her room was cushy and comfy. The morning sunlight streamed in to warm her and the air was sweetened by a bouquet of roses, compliments of the hotel manager. It was all fit for a princess. Yet she hadn't slept well.

Last night, as Juan Carlos bid her farewell, he'd almost kissed her. She was sure he would have if they hadn't been surrounded by his guests. She'd thought about that non-kiss during the night. How would his lips feel against hers? Heavens, she hadn't had so much as a date with a man in almost a year, and it had been even longer since she was ravaged by a kiss. Which, she was sure, would have happened had they been alone.

She was thankful that he hadn't locked lips with her in front of the attendees at the gala. Yet, lightbulbs had flashed and pictures had been snapped of the two of them. It was last thing she needed and she'd dashed out as rapidly as Cinderella racing against the midnight hour.

When he'd asked her to join him for brunch this morning, she'd quickly agreed, despite her tingling nerves and fuzzy brain.

Her brunch "date" with the King of Montoro would happen precisely at ten o'clock and he'd promised they wouldn't be interrupted.

She heard the familiar Bruno Mars ringtone of her cell phone and grabbed it from the nightstand. Her assistant's name popped up on the screen and she smiled. From the very beginning, her assistant had been her closest friend. "Hello, Jasmine."

"Hi, Portia. I hope I didn't wake you?"

"No, not at all. I'm getting ready to have brunch. It's good to hear your voice."

"Did you survive the coronation?" Jasmine Farr never minced words. "I know you weren't thrilled about attending."

"Actually, it wasn't so bad." The newly named king was quite a man. "And it's my lot in life to attend these functions every so often."

"That's what you get for being a princess." She chuckled. "I saw some of the coronation on YouTube."

"That was fast."

"It always is. Anyway, I'm calling to tell you that Mr. Greenboro had to cancel your meeting this week. He's flying out of the country and won't be back for three months. He sends his apologies, of course, and he did reschedule. I hope it's okay that I took the liberty of making that appointment. I didn't think you'd want to let him get away."

"Oh, I'm disappointed. I'd set the entire week aside to work with him, but I'm glad you're on the ball and rescheduled with him. Text me that date and I'll mark it on my calendar."

"Will do. So, now you don't have to rush back. There's really nothing else going on this week."

"Right."

"You've worked hard these past few months and you've been meaning to pencil in a vacation. Seems like a perfect opportunity."

"It is beautiful here."

"From the pictures I'm seeing, the beaches are to die for. I wish I could join you. I'd come in an instant."

"Why don't you come? We could have spa days together."

"I can't. I'm flying to Maryland for my cousin's wedding at the end of the week. "

"I'd forgotten about that. Darn."

"But that doesn't mean you can't stay on. I can book you a villa suite in Playa del Onda. The beach resort is top notch. You'll get lots of R&R."

"Let me think about it. I'll get back to you later on today."

After she ended the call, she stripped off her pajamas and entered the shower. The pounding water rained down and woke her up to the possibility of an actual vacation: away from phones, away from the hectic pace of gallery openings, away from the pressures of making art selections for her obscenely rich or drastically eccentric clients. Her schedule was a busy one, and this did seem like a perfect opportunity to unwind.

When she was finished with her shower, she slipped into a white dress with red polka dots that belted at the waist, slid on navy patent leather shoes and tossed her hair up into a ponytail. She applied light makeup, including eyeliner and soft pink lip gloss.

The jewelry she chose was delicate: a thin strand of pearls around her neck and wrist. She fastened her watch on her left arm and noted the time. Juan Carlos was sending a car for her in ten minutes. She grabbed her purse and left the hotel room.

In the lobby, she was greeted by a uniformed driver who escorted her to an ink-black limousine. She played the role of princess well, but she would rather be wearing a pair of jeans and going to the local café for a bite of breakfast.

"Your Highness," the driver said, as he opened the door for her, "allow me."

She slid into the backseat and bumped legs with Juan Carlos. Her breath hitched in her throat. He took in her wide-eyed surprise and grinned. "Good morning, Portia."

"Excuse me, but I didn't expect you to come to pick me up."

Should she worry about the implications? This wasn't a date. At least, not in any real sense.

"It's a nice morning for a drive. After yesterday's events, I thought you might like to join me to see some of the city. I hope you don't mind, but I've changed our brunch plans for today."

He wore dark slacks and a casual white silk shirt, opened slightly at the collar. She glimpsed his tanned chest and gulped for air.

"Of course not."

"Great. You look very pretty this morning."

"Thank you." *And you look dynamic, powerful and gorgeous.*

He issued directions to the driver and they took off.

"How were your first twenty-four hours as king?" she asked.

He rubbed his chin, thinking for a second. "It's strange that I don't feel any different. I keep expecting a big transformation, but I'm just me."

She smiled at his earnest answer. "I thought it would be an adjustment for you. Every move you make now will be documented somehow." She glanced out the window, expecting to see photographers following the limo, snapping pictures. She'd had experience with her ex-boyfriend's fame and it had gotten old very fast. No one should be followed and photographed at every turn for entertainment's sake. "How did you escape the palace?"

He chuckled. "You make it seem like prison."

"No, no. I'm sorry. That's not what I meant."

"I know what you meant, Portia." Her name slid effortlessly from his lips. "There are some advantages to being king."

"Such as?" she probed.

"Such as, I didn't make my intentions known. No one expected me to take a drive this morning. No one questioned me. I had the car ready to pick you up, and then I merely slipped into the backseat before anyone at the palace got wind of it."

"You snuck out."

He laughed again and she joined in. "Okay, yes. I snuck out."

Speaking to him put her at ease and she settled back in her seat. "Do you have bodyguards?"

"Yes, they are following behind somewhere."

"You're not worried?"

He shook his head. "No. I'm not worried. And neither should you be."

"Okay, I'll trust you." She'd never traveled with bodyguards, but her situation was quite different. As an exiled princess, she'd grown up in America and never had what Juan Carlos now had: a citizenry eager to reinstate their monarchy. "But you must have dozens of dignitaries and family members waiting to speak with you at the palace."

"Which I will do later. But for now," he said, reaching for her hand, "I find being with you more important."

Juan Carlos held her hand during the tour of the city. He showed her sites of great historical significance and some trendy new hot spots that were cropping up. The rise of democracy was good for enterprise, he explained.

As he spoke, the tone of his deep and sincere voice brought a smile to her lips more times than she could count. It was intimate in a way, hearing the love he had for a country that was almost as new to him as it was to her. He kept her hand locked in his as if it was precious. As if he needed the connection. To hear him say that being with her was important did wonders for her ego.

Yet she only indulged him because nothing could possibly come of it. And because it had been a long time since she'd enjoyed a man's company so much.

Tomorrow, she would leave Del Sol.

The limo stopped at a tiny café off the main street of town. "I hear Matteo's is fantastic."

"You've never eaten here before?" she asked.

"No, I haven't. We'll experience it together. Do you mind?"

"I love adventure."

He nodded, a satisfied glimmer in his eyes. "I thought you might."

They exited the limo, which looked out of place on the backstreets of the royal city. Once inside, they were escorted to their table by the owner. He was sweating, nervous and fidgety. Juan Carlos clapped him on the back gently to reassure him. "Bring us your specials, Matteo. I hear they are the best in all of Del Sol."

"*Si, si.* I will be glad to serve you myself, Your Majesty."

Juan Carlos nodded. "Thank you."

Though the café walls showed signs of age, it was a clean, modest place. "Are you sure the food is good here?" she asked.

His brows gathered. "It comes highly recommended. Why?"

"We're the only ones seated."

Juan Carlos looked around the empty café. "My bodyguards. They called ahead to announce my arrival. I'll make it up to Matteo. I can't have him losing business on my account."

"I'm sure he'll be boasting that King Montoro of Alma dined in his café. His business will double by next week."

Juan Carlos sharpened his gaze on her. "I hadn't thought of that."

"You're new to this royal thing."

"Yes, I guess I am."

Just wait, she wanted to say. He was an intelligent man, from all she'd read about him. He managed the sizable personal accounts of the Montoros and had helped build a fortune for the family. He had wits and smarts, but nothing would prepare him for the limelight he'd just entered. He'd have to experience it himself, the good, the bad, the ugly. His life would be under a microscope now.

And she didn't want to be the amoeba next to him.

Coffee was served, along with fresh handmade tortillas, butter and a bowl of cut fruit. "Looks delicious," Juan Carlos said to Matteo.

"Please, is there anything else I can bring you while the meal is cooking?"

"This is perfect. Don't you agree, Portia?"

She nodded and smiled at the owner.

When Matteo left the room she continued to smile. "You're kind. He will always remember this day because you put him at ease."

Travis Miles had been kind, too, in the beginning.

"Now who is being kind?" he asked.

"I'm just speaking the truth. You'll impact a great many lives."

"In a positive way, I hope and pray."

"Kind," she repeated. "You care about the people in the country."

"Thank you." His incredibly warm brown eyes softened and her stomach did a little flip.

She buttered a tortilla, rolled it up and took a few bites. She sipped coffee and asked Juan Carlos a few pointed questions about his life to keep the conversation flowing and her mind off the fact that King Montoro was a hunk.

The meal was delivered with fanfare. Matteo and his staff put out the dishes in sweeping motions and finally left them to dine privately. The food was delicious. The main dish consisted of bits of sautéed pork topped with eggs and lathered with a creamy, mildly spicy sauce. There was also some type of sweet corn soufflé served inside the husks, as well as caramelized plantains. Every bite she took rewarded her taste buds. "Mmm…this is heavenly."

Juan Carlos nodded, his mouth full.

As he chewed, his gaze remained on her. He had warm, luxurious, intense eyes that didn't stray. Goose bumps rode up and down her arms. As far as men went, Juan Carlos had it all, except for one thing. His fatal flaw. He was king. And that meant after today, she couldn't see him again.

"So what are your plans for the rest of the day?" he asked.

"Oh, I'm, uh, going to…" She really didn't have any plans. Maybe do a little shopping. Check out the only art museum in the city. "I'll be packing."

"That can't take all day."

"I wouldn't think so."

"Would you consider having dinner with me?"

No. No. No. "I really shouldn't."

Juan Carlos leaned back in his seat, studying her. "Do you have a man in your life, Portia?"

Slowly, she shook her head. She felt a trap coming.

"No one? I find that hard to believe. Do you date?"

"Rarely. My career is demanding. And it's very important to me. I've worked hard to get where I am."

"Admirable. Are you working tonight?"

"No, but I…"

He grinned. "I'm only asking for a dinner date, Portia."

Her shoulders sagged an inch. A barely noticeable move,

but she felt the defeat all the way down to her toes. She couldn't insult the king. "Then, yes, I'll have dinner with you."

After the meal, Juan Carlos escorted her to the limo. She took a seat at the far window and he climbed in after her. To his credit, he didn't crowd her, leaving a modest amount of space between them. But as the car took off, he placed his hand over hers on the empty seat, and wild pings of awareness shot through her body.

Don't let him get to you, Portia.

He's not the man for you.

As the limo pulled up to the hotel, Juan Carlos spoke to the driver. "Give us a minute please, Roberto."

The driver's door opened and closed quietly. Silence filled the air and suddenly she did feel crowded, though Juan Carlos hadn't made a move toward her. "I cannot walk you to your door, Princess."

"I understand."

"Do you? Do you know how much I want to?" His eyes were down, gazing at her hand as his thumb worked circles over her fingers. Her nerves jumped, like kernels of corn popping in a fry pan, one right after the other. "I don't want to cause you any inconvenience."

"I...know."

He tugged her hand gently and she fell forward, closing the gap between them. His dark-fringed eyelids lifted; she was struck by all-consuming heat. He wasn't moving a muscle, but leaving it up to her. As if she had a choice now. As if she could deny him. His mesmerizing hunger was contagious; years of abstinence made her hungry, as well. Her gaze lowered to his mouth. Lord in heaven, she wanted his kiss.

She moistened her lips and his eyes drew down immediately. "You leave me no choice, Princess."

He used a finger to tilt her chin, and then bent his head

toward her. Anticipation pulsed through her veins. Every single second was an unnerving kind of torture. And finally, his mouth was on hers, his hand coming to wrap more firmly around her jaw, as if he couldn't get enough, as if he would devour her.

Long live the king!

Her tummy ached from goodness and she indulged like a miser finding a hidden supply of cash. She touched his face, his jaw steel under her fingertips, and a groan erupted from his throat.

A whimpering mewling sound came from hers. Mortification would have set in, if the king wasn't equally as needy. But there was no shame, just honesty, and it was, after all, the kiss to end all kisses. Juan Carlos didn't let up, not for a moment. His lips worked hers hard, then soft, then hard again. Under her dress, her nipples ached. She was pretty sure the king was experiencing the same agony, but farther south on his body.

She didn't know whose mouth opened first, or whether it was at the exact same instant, but suddenly she was being swept up and hollowed out, his tongue doing a thorough job of ravaging her. Any second now, she'd be out of her head with lust. But Juan Carlos placed his hands on her shoulders and, she sensed, with great reluctance, moved her away from him.

He leaned back against the seat, breathing hard. "I've never made love to a woman in a limo before, Princess. It wouldn't take much to change that," he said. He tried for amusement, tried to chuckle, but a serious tone had given away his innermost thoughts.

"It would be a first for me, too," she said, coming up for air.

A rumpled mess, she tried her best to straighten herself out before she exited the limo.

He pressed a button and the window rolled down. Roberto appeared by the car door. "See Princess Portia to her hotel room," Juan Carlos said calmly. He'd gotten his emotions in check already, while she was still a ravaged jumble of nerves.

Again, those warm brown eyes lit upon her. "I'll send a car to pick you up for dinner at seven."

She swallowed. "Maybe…we shouldn't," she squeaked.

"Are you afraid of me?" he asked, though his confident tone indicated that it wasn't even a concern.

She shook her head. "I'm leaving in the morning."

"And you love your job. Your career means a lot to you. Yes, that's clear."

He'd made her refusal seem silly. And it was. Nothing would happen unless she wanted it to happen. She already knew Juan Carlos was that type of man.

"I'll see you tonight," she said finally. When the driver opened the car door, she rushed out.

She hadn't exactly lied to him, had she?

She said she'd be gone, and he thought she meant back to the States. But she'd made up her mind to vacation on the shores of Alma, at least until the end of the week.

But he didn't need to know that.

After a late lunch, Juan Carlos had a meeting in the city with the prime minister and few of Alma's most trusted and prominent business leaders. He struggled to keep his mind on the topics at hand. The restoration of the entire country was a tall order. But every so often, his mind traveled to that place where Portia was in his arms. The image of her lips locked on his, their bodies pulsing to the same lusty rhythms, knocked him for a loop and sent his brain waves scrambling. She was, in his estimation, perfect. For him. For the country.

Wow. Where had that come from? Why was he thinking of her in terms of permanence? As a queen for Alma, for goodness' sake.

Because aside from the fact that his sensual response was like the national flag being hoisted to full mast every time he looked at her, there was no doubt in his mind that she could take a place by his side at the throne.

As a public figure, he was never alone much anymore, but that didn't mean he wasn't lonely. He hadn't had a serious relationship for years. His ambition had gotten in the way and sure, he'd had a few women in his life, but nothing serious. No one who'd made him feel like this.

Portia's face flashed in his mind, that porcelain skin, those ice-blue eyes, that haughty chin, that mouth that tasted like sweet sin. The snow queen had become important to him in a short time, and...

"Your Majesty? Juan Carlos, are you all right?"

"Huh? Oh, yeah, I'm fine." Prime Minister Rivera was giving him a strange look. "Just deep in thought."

They'd been talking about how to bring new enterprise to Alma and how the rise of the monarchy would bring in tourism. They needed to brand themselves as a free country and show the world that democracy reigned, that new visitors and new businesses were welcome to their stunning Atlantic shores.

"Actually, I have an idea as to how to draw more tourists," Juan Carlos said.

"Really?"

Alex Ramon's ears perked up. As the deputy prime minister of commerce, he was fully immersed in the issue. "Tell us your thoughts."

"It's been rumored in our family for years that our ancestors had stashed a considerable amount of artwork, sculptures and paintings on land that had fallen to ruin. Land that Tantaberra overlooked. Right before the family was deposed, they'd thought to hide the art so it wouldn't fall into the dictator's greedy hands."

Juan Carlos's mind was clicking fast. He didn't know how true those rumors were. He'd only heard the tales while growing up; Uncle Rafael had spoken of hidden treasures the way a master storyteller would about a pirate's bounty. It had all been exciting, the sort of thing that captured a little boy's imagination. But the rumors had held fast and true during his adulthood, and only recently, his cousin Bella had found a hidden cache of letters at one of the family's abandoned farms, letters that proved that he, a Salazar and not a Montoro, was the rightful heir to the throne.

"I have plans to visit the area myself and see what I can find. If it's true, and artwork is indeed on the property, think of the story. The art could be restored, and we could have a special showing or a series of showings to bring awareness to Alma."

"It's genius, Your Highness," Prime Minister Rivera said.

Others around the board table agreed.

The meeting ran long and Juan Carlos didn't get back to the palace until six. He had just enough time to shower and dress for dinner. His pulse sped up as he thought of Portia again, of her sweetly exotic scent and the way she'd filled his body with pleasure when he was near her. She caused him to gasp and sweat and breathe hard. It wasn't ideal. She was a hard case. She didn't seem interested in him. And that worried him, because as far as he was concerned, she was The One.

He came down at precisely six forty-five and bumped into his new secretary at the base of the winding staircase, nearly knocking the clipboard out of her hands. "Oh, sorry, Your Highness." She was out of breath, as if she'd been running a marathon.

"My apologies," he said. "I've been preoccupied and didn't see you."

Alicia was redheaded, shapely and quite efficient. She wore glasses, but under those glasses were pretty, light green eyes. She'd taken on a lot, being a first hire, as there was much ground to cover. "Your seven o'clock appointment is here."

Warmth spread through his body at the mention of his dinner date. "Princess Portia?"

"Oh, uh. No, Your Highness. I'm sorry. I don't see Princess Portia on the books." She studied her clipboard, going over the names. "No, you have appointments every half hour for the next few hours. I penciled in a dinner break for you at nine."

"I thought those were on tomorrow night's schedule." Surely, he hadn't been mistaken, had he? Yet he had to take Alicia at her word. He'd already come to find that she rarely if ever made mistakes. He, on the other hand, had been hypnotized by a pair of deep ocean-blue eyes and was more than distracted.

"I can't possibly make all of those appointments." High-ranking officials and the heads of businesses along with their wives or husbands wanted to meet the new king. It was as simple as that. It was good for commerce to know the pillars of trade in Alma, so he'd agreed to a few evening appointments. Under normal circumstances, he'd rather cut off his right arm than cancel them, but he couldn't break a date with Portia. "See what you can do about cancelling them. Who was first on the schedule?"

"Mr. and Mrs. Rubino. The Rubinos are in the royal study. And your next appointment after that is already here, I'm afraid. They are notoriously early for every occasion, I'm told. They are waiting in the throne room."

He ran his hands through his hair. "Fine. I'll see them. But see what you can do about cancelling the rest."

"Yes, Your Highness. I'll do my best." She bit her lower lip, her eyes downcast. "Sorry for the confusion."

"Alicia?"

"Yes?"

"It's not your doing. I forgot about these appointments. We're all learning here. It's new to all of us."

She had ten years of experience running a duke's household in London, coordinating parties and events with dignitaries and the royal family. She hadn't much to learn. He was the one who had screwed up.

"Yes, Your Highness. I'll get on those cancellations right away."

Juan Carlos rubbed the back of his neck and headed to the study.

With luck, he could salvage the evening.

Portia had been stood up. She'd been delivered to the palace minutes before seven, only to be informed that the king had visitors and to please be patient and wait. She was shown to the dining room and shortly after, the palace chef himself had set dishes of appetizers on the table before her.

Candles were lit and soft music filtered into the room.

The only problem? Her date wasn't here. And she wasn't about to eat a thing until he showed. Call her stubborn.

It was after eight. She knew because her stomach refused to stop growling and finally, she'd glanced at her watch.

She'd already taken in the paintings on the walls, assessing them and noting that they weren't up to par with usual palatial art. Oh, they were lovely pieces, but from contemporary artists. Many of them were replicas of the real thing. It was a curiosity. The monarchy stretched way beyond the years of the dictatorship. There should be older, more authentic works on the walls. But this was only one room. Maybe for security reasons, the gallery held the most valuable pieces.

After wandering the dining hall, she picked a particular patch of space near the fireplace and began pacing.

She couldn't fault Juan Carlos. His secretary had taken the blame, explaining that she'd failed to remind the king of his visitors. She'd tried her best to cancel the meetings, but she was afraid she wasn't as successful as she'd hoped.

But the more Portia thought about it, the more pangs of anger replaced her patience.

How long would he keep her waiting?

Travis is in a meeting. He won't be available for hours. He'd like you to wait, though.

This isn't the same thing, she reminded herself. Her ex-boyfriend wasn't a king. Well, maybe the king of late-night television. And she'd fallen for him. He was funny and charming and kind. It was like a regular Cinderella story, the poor broke comedian hooks up with a real live princess. Travis was far from poor now, although he'd come from humble beginnings and the press loved their story and ate it up.

A new American fairy tale, they'd called it.

Travis had been on top of the world when they were together. Everyone loved him and thought he was worthy of a princess from an obscure little country. Only dating a supermodel would have given him more credibility.

And here she was, doing the same thing. Another American fairy tale, only this time with a real king.

Stupid of her.

Her nerves were jumpy and by the time eight-thirty rolled around, she was royally pissed.

Juan Carlos had twisted her arm to accept this dinner date, the way charming men did. He'd trapped her and then kissed her until every brain cell was lulled into capitulation. God, she'd been looking forward to being alone with him again. That kiss was good. Better than good. It was the best kiss she'd ever had. Not even Travis could kiss like that, and he'd been plenty experienced in that department.

"Sorry, so sorry, Portia."

She jumped. "Oh!" Juan Carlos entered the room, looking dashing in a dark buttoned-up suit but no tie. Another growl emitted from her stomach, this time not due to hunger.

"Did Alicia explain what happened? It was my fault. This is the first chance I've had to—"

"It's been over ninety minutes," was all she could think to say.

"I would've cancelled with you and sent you home, but this is your last night in Alma. Selfishly, I wanted to see you again."

Guilt rose like bile in her throat. She remained silent.

He glanced at the feast of food that had been put before her. "You didn't touch anything Chef prepared. You must be famished."

"I'm not hungry anymore, Your Majesty."

His lips pursed in disapproval.

She still couldn't bring herself to call him by his given name.

"You've been so patient. There's just one more meeting I have to get through. Will you wait?"

She shook her head. "Actually, I think I'd like to go."

"You're angry."

"No, I'm tired and, and…"

"Angry."

She didn't respond. "Will you have your driver take me back to the hotel?"

Juan Carlos closed his eyes briefly. "Yes, of course. I just assumed after we kissed, you'd… Never mind. You're right. I shouldn't have made you wait."

A man who admitted when he was wrong? How rare.

"Duty called. I'm afraid it always will."

That's how it had worked with Travis. The difference? Travis had been building his own personal dynasty, while Juan Carlos was trying to build one for his country. But that still left Portia with the same end result. She'd never be a top priority and while she liked Juan Carlos, she had vowed, after many disappointments with Travis, to never get herself in that situation again.

With that, she wished Juan Carlos a good evening, assured him she wasn't angry and put enough distance between them that he couldn't touch her, couldn't plant his delicious lips on hers again and make her change her mind.

Three

The beach at Playa del Onda was one of the most stunning Portia had ever visited. Warm sand squeezed between her toes as she sat on a lounge chair, reading a book. This morning she'd gotten up early and taken a long jog along the shoreline, the October sun warming her through and through. She'd met a lovely family of tourists and had breakfast with them at a terrace café that overlooked the Atlantic. But their two little children, aged five and three, reminded her that it would probably be a long time before she was blessed with motherhood.

Often, she thought of having a family. She'd been orphaned at a young age. Aside from her great-aunt Margreta, she had no other family. Her grandmother Joanna had died during Portia's sophomore year in college. But she had her work and it fulfilled her, and she had good friends. She wasn't complaining. Yet being here on this beautiful beach was not only relaxing, it was…lonely.

Face it, Portia. How many books can you read this week? How many hot stone spa treatments can you indulge in? How many solo dinners in your room can you enjoy?

It had been three days of torturous relaxation. And it didn't compute. How odd for her to realize while on a vacation in a beautiful locale that she wasn't made for inactivity. She liked to keep active, to busy herself with things that mattered. Yesterday, she'd given herself a mental slap.

You deserve this vacation, so shut up, sit back and enjoy yourself.

Today, the mental slaps weren't working. Her relaxation was even more forced. She fidgeted in her chair; the book in her hands no longer held her interest. Sunglasses shading her eyes, she watched others frolicking on the sand, tossing a Frisbee, their laughter drifting over to her, reminding her how lonely she was. How bored.

She wished Jasmine was here. They would've had a good time with shopping, spa dates and maybe a nightclub or two.

The Frisbee landed at her feet and a teenage boy trotted over and stopped abruptly, blasting sand onto her legs. "Excuse me," he said. He reached for the Frisbee slowly, eyeing her legs, then her bikini-clad body. "Want to play with us?" he asked.

He had Spanish good looks, dark hair, bronzed skin and a charming smile. He was sixteen tops, and she would've actually considered tossing the Frisbee around with him, if he hadn't been so blatant about ogling her breasts.

She was saved from refusing, when the concierge from the Villa Delgado approached. "Excuse me, Princess."

The boy blinked at her title, turned a lovely shade of cherry-blossom pink and bowed, before dashing off. She chuckled under her breath. Her royal status did have some advantages. "Yes," she said to the concierge, removing her sunglasses.

"You have a phone call at the desk. A woman named Jasmine. She says she works for you. Apparently, she hasn't been able to reach you on your cell phone."

"I left my cell in my room," she replied. She didn't want to be interrupted in her state of lonely boredom. Now she realized how silly that seemed. "Sorry you had to track me down."

"Not a problem, Princess Portia."

"Will you tell her that I'll call her as soon as I get to my room?"

"My pleasure," he said.

When he walked off, she gathered up her beach bag, hat and sunglasses and promptly made her way toward the villa. Her suite with its second-floor terrace came into view. It was really quite picturesque, the columns and archways suggesting old-world grace and style. Why couldn't she like being here more? Why wasn't she okay with being idle? Maybe things had changed with Jasmine. Maybe her friend would come join her, after all. Her hope in her throat, Portia hiked a little faster to reach her suite of rooms.

Once inside, she set her things down on the dining table and headed for the bedroom, where she was sure she'd left her phone. It was charging on her nightstand. She unhooked the charger, just as she heard a knock at the door.

She belted her cover-up a little tighter and moved to the door. With a gentle tug on the knob, the door opened and she came face to face with Juan Carlos Salazar. The king.

She blinked and a rush of heat rose up her neck. She trembled at the sight of him, *the gorgeous, unexpected, surprising* sight of him. The phone slipped slightly in her hand and she grabbed at it before it crashed onto the floor.

His eyes were on her, and those dark raised brows made her flush even hotter. With guilt. Piercing disappointment flickered in his eyes. She hadn't told him the absolute truth when she'd left Del Sol.

"Princess," he said.

"Your Majesty," she responded.

His lips twitched. "I see you've decided to stay on in Alma, after all."

"I, uh, yes." She didn't owe him an explanation. One heart-robbing kiss didn't give him that right. "My plans changed."

"Quite unexpectedly, I assume."

"Yes, that's right." The movement of two bodyguards caught her attention. They stayed back, at least five feet away, but she was certain they could hear every word. "Would you like to come in?"

His gaze dipped down to her bikini-clad body, covered only by a soft robe of silk that reached her thighs. "Yes."

She backed up a few steps and he nodded to his bodyguards and then entered. They stood face-to-face again, alone in her suite.

Despite her guilt and a sense of being caught redhanded, this was the most exciting thing that had happened to her in three days. But how did he find out where she was and what did he want from her?

Her cell phone buzzed and she looked down at the screen. A text was coming through from Jasmine. She hadn't had time to call her back yet. Quickly, she scanned the message.

Heads up. I might've made a mistake by giving King Montoro your location. He was charming and said it was a business thing. Apologizing in advance. Love you!

She lifted her lids to him. Okay, so he wasn't psychic. But he was thorough.

"It's good to see you again," he said.

Warmth swelled inside her like an overflowing river. He had too much of an effect on her.

"It's nice to see you, but I do admit, it's quite a surprise."

On this warm day, he was wearing dark trousers and a tan shirt, sleeves rolled up with his hands in his pockets, looking as casual and delicious as any man she'd ever met. Man, *not king.* But she couldn't forget who he was. "I have to admit, I was also surprised to learn you hadn't left the country."

"You were looking for me?"

"Yes, I spoke with your assistant. She's very nice, by the way, and she's loyal to you. But the fact is, I have something of a business venture for you. And after I told her a little about it, she was willing to let me get in touch with you."

His eyes skimmed over Portia's body. Another wave of heat shimmied down to her belly and she turned away from his hot, assessing stare. Man or king, he was dangerous. "Would you like to sit down?" She waved him over to a latte-colored leather chair by the window that faced the Atlantic. "Please give me a minute to change my clothes."

"Only if you have to."

There was a wicked twinkle in his eyes that tweaked something lusty and recently unleashed in her body. It made her run, not walk toward her bedroom. "I'll be a minute, Your Majesty," she called over her shoulder.

His chuckle followed her into her room.

She scrubbed her face clean of sunscreen and removed her hair fastener, combing the tangles away and then gathering the strands back up into a long ponytail. She put on a pair of white capris and an off-the-shoulder cornflower-blue blouse.

A hint of lip gloss, some shading to her eyelids and she was ready. And more than mildly curious as to what was so important that King Juan Carlos had come all the way here to seek her out. She gave a last glance in the mirror and nodded. She felt a little less vulnerable to the king's hungry eyes now.

Juan Carlos stood when Portia entered the room. His heart hammered in his chest at the sight of her. She didn't know it yet, but he was determined to possess her. Aside from his newfound reign over Alma and his duties here, she'd become the most important thing in his life.

In such a short time.

It wasn't rational. He had no explanation for it. He'd never experienced anything quite like this. When she'd left the palace the other night, remorse had plagued him and lingered for days. Was he pathetic? Or simply a man who knows what he wants.

She was perfect, his ideal woman. She was royal, beautiful, smart, but at the moment…quite unattainable.

"Princess," he said.

"Would you like something cold to drink?" she asked.

"No, thank you."

"Okay, then maybe we should sit down and you can tell me what this is all about."

She took a seat, her eyes widening as she waited for him to explain.

"It seems I might have need for your services."

"My services? As an art advisor?"

"Well, yes. In a way. It would be something quite adventurous. You did say you liked adventure, didn't you?"

"I do."

"Well, then, let me explain. I don't know how much you know about the history of Alma, but it's been rumored that right before my family fled the country, they hid artwork dating back before World War II on the grounds of their abandoned farm. It's very run-down and Tantaberra never went there, so it was the perfect hiding place. Now that I'm king, I want to find those treasured pieces belonging to the royal family. It would go a long way in helping the country heal and bring new hope to our people. Imagine what a find that would be."

"It would be monumental," she agreed. Fireworks lit in her eyes at the mention of hidden art.

Good. He had her attention.

"But I see that you're vacationing here, so maybe you'd be too busy to help me locate the treasure."

"You want my help in locating the artwork?"

"Yes, I would need someone to help me hunt for it, and then assess its value. You'd be able to look at something and determine if it's authentic, I would imagine."

"Yes, for the most part. It's what I do. But you plan on doing this by yourself?"

"I can donate a few days of my time, yes. I wouldn't want word to leak out about what I was doing. If I come up empty, or if there are other issues regarding the artwork we find, I would rather it not become public knowledge immediately. Bella and her husband had already begun renovations on the property but given the site's historical significance, they've agreed to allow me to take over and devote the full resources of the crown to the project. As we speak, there is a team working on the grounds, getting it ready for my arrival. So Princess Portia, would you consider helping me? Of course, you'd be paid for your time."

"So, this is a job offer?"

"Yes, I'm offering you a job and an adventure."

She smiled, leaning forward and placing her hands on her crossed knee. "Who else will be there?"

He gathered his brows. "No one but my bodyguards. As I said, I plan to do this discreetly."

"It's intriguing, Your Majesty. But the two us alone, all that time?"

"Is that a problem for you?" God only knew, it was a problem for him. How could he keep his hands off her? It would be a living hell, but not worse than having her living a continent away. A few days was all he was asking of her.

"Maybe. Answer one thing for me, please."

He extended his arms, palms up. "Anything."

"Do you have an ulterior motive in offering me this opportunity? And please don't make me spell it out."

He smiled. She'd made her point and he wouldn't do her a disservice by lying to her. "If you mean, do I value a few more days in your company, then yes. I suppose. But I do honestly have good reason to be asking this of you. You are an expert, are you not?"

"I am."

The sparkle in her eyes evaporated.

"What is it?"

She rose from her seat, and good manners had him rising, too. She walked behind the chair, putting distance between them, and leaned her elbows on the back, a battle raging in her eyes, on her face. "I'm not presuming anything here, but I do have to tell you where I stand. It's... it's complicated. Because I do like you."

Encouraging. He nodded.

"And that kiss we shared...well, it bordered on amazing."

He nodded again. She had something to say and he wanted to hear it.

Or maybe not.

"But the truth is, you're King Montoro of Alma. You're new to this king thing, but you'll find out how demanding a job it will be. And you'll be in the spotlight. All. The. Time."

"Does that worry you?"

"Yes. You see, I'm not one to share heartbreak stories, but in this case, I should probably share with you, why I've been—"

"Playing hard to get?" He couldn't hold back a smile.

"Yes. Only I'm not playing. I'm seriously not interested in getting involved with a man with so much...glitter."

"Glitter?" He laughed. "What's that?"

"You're always going to shine. No matter what." His smile faded. She was dead serious. "And any woman who gets involved with you, will be giving up her identity, her dreams, her heart, to someone who has pledged his life to his country."

"Who was he, Portia? Surely, someone has broken your heart."

"Yes, my heart was broken. I don't like talking about it, but since it's important to our conversation, I'll tell you about Travis Miles. He's like a king in America, a big time Hollywood celebrity."

Juan Carlos nodded. "Of course I know of him. I don't go in much for entertainment news, but he sure has quite a résumé."

"Travis knows everyone of substance in the country from sports figures and superstars to high-ranking politicians. We ran hot for a short time, and then…I became old news to him. He didn't have time for me and we began seeing less and less of each other. Shortly after, I found out he'd been cheating on me with a woman on the staff of his TV show for a long time. Seems that everyone knew about it but poor little gullible me. He'd made me out to be a fool and my career and credibility suffered. It's taken me three years to get my reputation back. Princess or not, I wasn't immune to the blonde-bimbo stigma and so now, I'm cautious. Which is why your royal status isn't a plus in my book."

He stood with hands on hips, silent, taking it all in. He understood her caution. The pain in her eyes, the tremor in her voice were telling, and his heart hurt hearing her confession. He should leave and let her resume her vacation. He shouldn't press her. But his feet were planted and they weren't moving. He couldn't face not seeing her again.

"If things were different, would you accept my offer?"

"Yes," she said, her eyes clear now. "I wouldn't hesitate. It sounds far too exciting to pass up."

"Then let's pretend that we've just met. There was no amazing kiss from before. We haven't danced and spent time together. This is a business meeting. And I promise to keep things completely professional between us."

"Why is it so important to you?" she asked.

"Because, I…I see how much you want to say yes. I see that you'd love to locate the secret artworks."

"And you promise that after we discover this wonderful treasure, we'll just be friends?"

He let a split second go by. He was a man of his word.

If he promised, he'd have to adhere to his vow, regardless of how much he wanted things to be different.

"I promise, Princess."

She nodded. "I know you mean what you say. So yes, I accept your offer."

The next morning, Portia informed the concierge that she'd be checking out earlier than expected from Villa Delgado and offered her thanks for his accommodations. He'd questioned her, hoping she hadn't been disappointed in her stay, and she assured him that was not the case. She'd been called away unexpectedly, she explained. And his brows arched as if he'd suspected King Montoro had something to do with her sudden departure.

And so, her adventure was beginning. Dressed for the search, wearing a pair of Gucci jeans and a red plaid shirt tucked in and belted at the waist, she swopped out her Bruno Magli shoes for tall leather boots and stood outside the villa at precisely eight o'clock. Sunglasses shielding her eyes, her bags packed and ready to go, she gave one last glance to the Atlantic shoreline and the clear azure waters lapping the sands. There would be no five-star accommodations where she was going. She was told to expect rustic and that was fine with her. She'd gone camping before; she knew how to rough it.

Sort of. Jasmine had convinced her once to rent a motor home and they'd trekked as far as Pismo Beach, California. They'd parked the giant thing facing the ocean, and then had gone out for lunch and dinner every night. They'd hit a few clubs, too, dancing until dawn. So maybe that wasn't roughing it per se.

But they had cooked their own breakfasts and hiked the beach in the mornings. Did that count?

One of Juan Carlos's bodyguards drove up in a black SUV, right on time. Poker-faced, he promptly opened the door for her and she got into the backseat as he hoisted her luggage into the cargo space.

As they drove off, she sat quietly in the car, enjoying the sounds of morning, excitement flowing through her veins.

She'd taken Juan Carlos at his word. He would treat her as a professional and so she had nothing to fear and everything to look forward to. Her little heartfelt speech seemed to convince him that she wasn't looking for romantic involvement. Surprisingly, it hadn't been hard admitting her failings to him. He'd put her at ease and that was saying something, since she didn't go around revealing her innermost feelings to anyone but her best friend.

They drove away from the shore, through the streets of Playa del Onda and onto a highway that led inland. "Excuse me. When will we be picking up King Montoro?" she asked Eduardo, the driver-slash-bodyguard.

"His Majesty will be meeting you there," he said.

Ah…discretion.

"Is it a long drive?"

"Not overly so. We should arrive in less than an hour. Is there anything you need, Princess?"

"No, no. I'm perfectly comfortable."

She gazed out the window taking in the scenery, where residential streets were soon replaced by more rural-looking spaces. As the minutes ticked by, the groomed vegetation bordering the road gave way to untamed brush and wildflowers. There was a certain neglected beauty to the land that inspired her. The road though was becoming less and less car friendly. The tires spit broken gravel as they traveled along a bumpy country road.

"Sorry, Princess," Eduardo said. "The road is washed out from here on."

"Is it much longer?"

"No, just another mile or two."

And shortly, he turned onto a path and drove through

wrought-iron gates clawed by fingers of dead branches and vines. Weeds and overgrown scrub led to a two-story house in desperate need of a good solid paint job. Banging sounds reached her ears and she searched for the source as the car came to a stop in front of the house. Juan Carlos appeared on the porch holding a hammer, his shirt slung open and sweat glistening on his beautiful bronzed chest. His dark hair gleaming under the October sunshine, he gave her a wide welcoming smile.

She sucked oxygen in. If she could slither away in a trembling mass, she would. She could order Eduardo to turn the car around, drive and keep on driving until she forgot the exact chestnut color of Juan Carlos's eyes, the deep dark shine of his hair and the powerful rock-solid muscle of his body.

She bit her lower lip until it pained her.

As he made his approach, she bucked up and remembered why she was here, and the promise Juan Carlos had made to her. Now, if she could get her heart to stop racing…

"Welcome," he said, opening the door wide for her. He offered her his hand and helped her out of the car. Eyes shining, his smile broadened. "I hope your trip wasn't too uncomfortable."

"No, no. It was fine," she said, looking beyond him to the house.

"Sorry about my appearance."

She nearly choked on her own saliva. Was he kidding?

"I found some loose planks on the porch. They could be dangerous."

"You're handy with a hammer?"

"You sound surprised. Actually, I had a lot of odd jobs in my younger days. My uncle believed in hard work and I was always employed during my college years."

"Doing?"

"All sorts of things. Remind me to tell you about the time I worked at a strip club in Miami."

"You were a stripper?"

The image of him shedding his clothes made her mouth water.

"I didn't say that. But I sure got a quick education." Her eye fluttered and he squeezed her hand. "There's that wink again. I'm very happy you're here, Portia."

"It's not a wink," she assured him.

He smiled again and released her hand. Breath quietly swooshed out of her mouth.

"Let me assure you, the inside of the house is in better shape than the outside. Bella and James had two bedrooms renovated upstairs and my crew made sure the kitchen and living space are clean and functioning."

She flinched at the mention of the bedrooms and slid a glimpse at Eduardo, who was removing her luggage, appearing stoic as ever. "That's…fine."

She only wished that Juan Carlos would button his shirt so that she could breathe freely again.

Eduardo stopped at the steps with her two suitcases. "Just leave them. I'll take it from here," Juan Carlos said. "Thanks, Eduardo."

The man nodded, but it looked more like a bow. "Your Highness."

Juan Carlos rolled his eyes.

She chuckled. It would take him a while to get used to being royalty.

"Stop laughing," he whispered out of earshot of his bodyguard.

"I'll try," she whispered back. "Not promising anything."

He shook his head but grinned like a schoolboy.

She was up against massive charm and a killer body.

"Let me show you around." Juan Carlos took her arm and guided her inside.

The living room was cozy with a large brick fireplace and old wood floors that looked as though they'd been scoured and polished. A new patterned rug was laid down between two sofas covered with floral tapestry pillows. The smell of fresh drying paint filled the room.

"Come see the kitchen," he said, taking her hand. "It's rustic, but I didn't have the heart to replace everything. I'm assured the oven is in working order." The oven was indeed, quaint and lovely. She could tell it, too, had been scoured to a new brilliance, but it must date back to the 1940s. The refrigerator had been replaced, and the counters were chipped in places but the sink had passed the test of time. A kitchen table sat in front of windows overlooking the backyard grounds. Someone had recently plowed the area and planted a garden of fresh flowers and herbs so the immediate view was quite picturesque.

"It's charming the way it is."

"The refrigerator is stocked. Would you like a cold drink?"

"Sure."

He opened the door and peeked inside. "Lemonade, soda, orange juice and sparkling water."

"Lemonade sounds good. I'll get the glasses." She flipped open a few cupboards and found them. It was obvious the dinnerware and glassware were all new, or imported from the palace. "Here we go." She set two glasses in front of him on the counter and he filled them.

A cool, refreshing swallow quenched her thirst and as she sipped, she strolled through the kitchen, exploring. She passed a utility room and then entered a large bathroom. Juan Carlos was just steps behind her and prickles of awareness climbed up her spine. She felt his eyes on her and as she turned slowly, he didn't even try to look away. He was in the doorway, his arms braced on the doorjamb, his shirt hanging open loosely from his shoulders. All that pure masculinity in one man didn't seem fair.

He stared at her for long seconds, until regret seemed to dull the gleam in his eyes. She had the same regret. If only she was just a woman and he was just a man and they were here together, sharing a grand adventure.

She swiveled around, pretending interest in a claw-foot tub, running a finger along the porcelain edge. "Makes you wonder about what life was like here when the farm was active." She turned to him again. "Do you know if there were animals?"

"Hmm. I think so. There are many outer buildings on the acreage. Supply sheds, barns and feed shacks. They owned livestock. Probably sheep, maybe cattle, but definitely horses. Do you ride?"

"Horses? Yes, I do. I'm no expert but I know how to plant my butt in the saddle."

He smiled.

"Will we be riding?"

"Possibly. There's five thousand acres here to investigate. Between the Jeep and the horses, we should be able to scour the entire grounds. The horses will be here this afternoon."

"Did your family ever live here?"

"I don't think a Salazar ever lived here. But a Montoro must have at some point. This land is all part of the Montoro holdings."

"Do you have any idea where to start looking?"

"I'm thinking we should stick close to the house today and if we come up empty, we can venture out tomorrow."

"Sounds good. I have to admit, I'm eager to start."

"Okay, then I'll get your luggage. Your room is upstairs at the end of the hallway. It's been painted and furniture was brought in yesterday. Take some time to relax. I think you'll like the room, but if there's anything you need, just let me know."

"I'm sure it's fine." She'd roughed it with Jasmine, after

all. She really could handle her own luggage, but His Majesty would never allow that. His sense of gentlemanly duty would become tarnished. And darn, if she didn't find that amazingly appealing. "Thank you."

As she headed upstairs, a sigh escaped from her lips.

Juan Carlos was a big juicy ripe apple, dangling his unabashed charm and beautiful body in front of her.

And the wicked serpent in her head was daring her to take a bite.

Four

Portia's room was more than adequate. A queen-size bed, adorned with Egyptian cotton sheets, a snowy comforter and pale pink pillows took up most of the space. Southern light streamed into the room through twin windows with ruffled curtains and an exquisitely crafted armoire made of inlaid mahogany and cherrywood held the bulk of her clothes.

She glanced out one window to the unkempt grounds below. The Montoros owned all the land as far as her eyes could see. Would they find the hidden artwork somewhere out there? Her belly warmed to the idea. She was grateful for the opportunity to search for it.

And ready.

As she headed for the stairs, movement caught her eye from a room at the opposite end of the landing. Juan Carlos was in his bedroom, changing his shirt. Twenty feet separated them, and she immediately glanced away, but not before she caught sight of bare broad shoulders tapering down to a trim waist. She gulped and scurried down the stairs before she got caught ogling him.

She wandered outside into the yard. Birds flitted between tree branches and flew away. She knew the bodyguards were out here somewhere, watching over the place, but she'd yet to see anyone else since Eduardo had deposited her here this morning.

She heard the door open and close behind her and footsteps crunching the fallen leaves as Juan Carlos approached. "Where are they? I know they are out there somewhere," she said.

He chuckled. "Luis and Eduardo have orders not to disturb us unless there's danger. They're here, trust me."

"I'm not worried." She put on a pair of sunglasses.

"That's good. How do you like your room?" He sidled up next to her. Dressed in jeans and a chambray shirt, with a black felt hat shading his eyes, he looked like a modern-day Spanish vaquero.

"It's better than I imagined, considering the state of the grounds around us. I'm sure you had a hand in making it comfortable for me."

He shrugged. "If you're comfortable, that's all that matters. Let's check out what we can on foot. There's a stable and a few broken-down buildings nearby." He reached into his back pocket and came up with a pair of work gloves. "Here, put these on."

She slipped them on. "I'm ready." And off they went.

The stable was in ruins, like pretty much everything else on the property. As they entered, she spied a wagon wheel, some rusted harnesses and a stack of rotted grain bags. It didn't seem as though anything could be hidden in here, but Juan Carlos touched every wall, kicked clean every stall and scoured the entire area with assessing eyes.

She took his cue, and searched the outside perimeter of the building, looking for anything that could be used as a hiding place.

He met her outside. "Nothing here. I didn't think we'd find anything this close to the house, but we need to be thorough."

"Okay, where next?"

"There's some feed shacks farther out we should check. Are you up for a long walk?"

She stared into his eyes. "You know that pea under my mattress didn't ruin my sleep last night."

He gave her a look of mock concern. "There was a pea under your mattress, Princess? Twenty lashes for the chambermaid who made up your bed last night."

She grinned. "More like fifty lashes for the king who thinks I can't keep up with him."

"Okay, I get your point. You're not frail."

"Not one little bit. But I think your concern is sweet."

"And antiquated."

"That, too. But what woman doesn't dream of a knight in shining armor once in a while?"

He peered directly into her eyes. "Do you?"

"I'm…not going to tell."

With that, she dashed ahead of him and hoped she was heading in the right direction.

Juan Carlos's laughter reached her ears, but he hung back a little, watching her.

She came upon three outer buildings, each one fifty feet or so from the others. She was just about to enter one when Juan Carlos called out, "Portia, wait!"

She whirled around. He came marching toward her, making up their distance in long strides. "Let's do this together."

He was being overprotective again. "I don't see why I can't—"

"Humor me," he said, sweeping up her hand and tugging her inside with him.

The small shed was in better shape than the stable had been. Juan Carlos remarked on how it was a newer building, perhaps added on later as the farm prospered. The open door allowed a sliver of light inside the windowless and otherwise dark space. Juan Carlos released her hand and the tingles streaming down her arm finally eased.

He got down on his knees and scoured the floorboards, looking for a trap door while she tapped at the walls. She tugged at a splintered hoe leaning against the far wall, moving it out of her way. A deafening hiss broke the silence. She looked down and saw a snake coiling around her boot. Panicking, she gasped quietly.

Juan Carlos jumped up. "Don't move!"

She froze. Oh, God, no. "What should I do? What should I do?" The thing was moving up her leg.

"Hold still, sweetheart. Trust me."

Juan Carlos reached into his boot and a glint of silver caught her eye. A knife?

There was a flash of movement as he lunged forward, and she squeezed her eyes shut. He ripped the thing off her in seconds flat. When she opened her eyes, she saw that he'd slashed the snake's neck all the way through. Juan Carlos tossed the dead reptile, head and all, across the shed. It landed with a smack and her stomach recoiled.

She shook uncontrollably and Juan Carlos took her into his arms. "You're okay, Portia. You're okay, sweetheart."

Tears spilled from her eyes and she nodded.

"Let's get outside," he said softly.

"I don't know if I can move."

"You can. I'll help you."

She nodded. "Okay." She clung to him as he guided her into the daylight. Fresh air filled her lungs and helped with her shaking.

"I'm sorry," he said, over and over, kissing her forehead.

She held his neck tight. She'd never been so frightened in her life. It all happened so fast, but the thought of that thing crawling up her body would surely give her nightmares for days to come.

"No, she'll be fine. I've got this," he was saying to someone, shaking his head. Then he turned his attention back to her. "Sweetheart, we'll go back to the house now."

"Who were you talking to?" She glanced past his shoulders and caught Eduardo gazing at her for a second before he lowered his eyes.

"We can walk, unless you want Eduardo to drive us back to the house?"

"No." She clung to Juan Carlos tighter, still shocked. She wasn't ready to let go. "No, we have more to do."

He ran his hand over her ponytail, like a father would a child. "But not today, Portia." His voice was gentle. "Not if you're not up to it."

She glanced to where Eduardo had been standing. He'd disappeared.

"Just hold me a little longer, please."

"Of course." One hand ran comforting circles on her back.

"I…I guess you have your answer." She spoke into his shirt, still too freaked out to back away.

"What do you mean?"

"You're my knight in shining armor today."

"Just today?" There was amusement in his voice and Portia couldn't deny how safe she felt being in his protective arms.

"Hmm." To say more would be too revealing. She was vulnerable right now and had let her guard down with him. She didn't want to let go of him. She needed his strength. He bolstered her courage.

"I guess, I'll settle for that," he said.

She tipped her chin up and gazed into his eyes. It would be so easy to kiss him now, to thank him for saving her from that creature.

"Portia," he whispered. His gaze tumbled down to her lips and the longing in his voice tortured her.

Debating with herself, she closed her eyes.

She heard him sigh deeply as one hand gripped her shoulders. He gave a little shove and she stumbled back and then blinked. He'd set her away deliberately. She focused on the blade he still held in his other hand and the image of that snake's split body flashed again in her mind.

A tick worked at his jaw, beating an erratic rhythm. "You test my honor, Portia. I made you a promise."

"I...know."

He put his head down, not meeting her eyes, and then bent to wipe the blade clean on the grass. One, two, three slashes were all that he needed. Then he stood and sheathed the knife, placing it in his waistband. "Come," he said, reaching for her gloved hand. "We should go."

"Yes. I can make it to the other shacks now."

He nodded and led the way.

"Here." Juan Carlos set a glass of whiskey into her hand. "Take a few sips and drink slowly." She sat on the sofa near the fireplace and kept her eyes focused on the jumping blue-orange flames. They sizzled and popped and brought warmth to the cool evening. "You'll need it to calm down."

"I'm calm." She wasn't really. Her body still quaked inside even as she sipped the numbing whiskey. The thought of that snake wrapped around her made her stomach curl. Yuck, it was disgusting. And frightening. Juan Carlos had been wonderful. He'd stayed by her side and comforted her, and hadn't balked when she'd insisted on continuing on their search. Though he'd made a thorough check of the next two buildings for creatures before he allowed her to step foot inside. He'd told her he was proud of her. It hadn't been courage on her part, but rather sheer stubborn determination that made her put one foot in front of the other and kept her from running back to the house for refuge. They hadn't found a thing in those other sheds, not one clue as to the whereabouts of the treasure, and she'd been ridiculously happy to return to the house after they'd exhausted their foot search.

"How's that going down?" he asked.

"Smooth. I'm not usually a hard drinker."

"But you needed something tonight."

"I'm not usually such a wimp, either," she said, smiling awkwardly. She'd felt like an idiot for panicking after Juan Carlos explained that the snake probably wasn't poisonous or deadly, but her fear was real, and he'd understood that. Rather than take a chance, he'd done the manly thing. He'd killed the culprit. Her knight.

"You were very brave. You kept your cool."

"You mean I froze in panic?"

He stared at her from his perch atop the sofa arm. "I'm sorry you had to go through that. I promise nothing like that will ever happen to you again. I'm very cautious. I'll take care to secure the site before you go pouncing."

"I don't *pounce*," she said.

"Don't you?" He smiled over his glass and sipped whiskey. "I had to stop you from going inside by yourself."

"I didn't know there would be snakes."

He arched his brows. "All the more reason for us to stick closer together."

"Can't get much closer than this," she said, chuckling. Oh, but yes, they could, and Juan Carlos's arched brow, the amusement in his eyes, said he was thinking the same thing. The thought of sleeping just down the hall from him tonight killed her laughter. The alcohol was already affecting her brain, and her rational thinking. She set her glass down, looking into the amber liquid that remained. She needed her wits about her. It would be too easy to fall into lust with the king. "I think I'll be okay now. What's the plan for tomorrow?"

He thought about it a few seconds. "Tomorrow, we go out on horseback. There's some terrain I want to explore that we can't get to with the Jeep."

"Are the horses here?"

He nodded. "They arrived this afternoon. Eduardo and Luis have stabled them."

"You've thought of everything, Your Highness."

"Juan Carlos."

She grinned. "I'm sorry. Still can't get there."

He shrugged, and it dawned on her that she needed that wall of separation in order to remind herself who he was. She'd do better to think of him as a monarch, rather than a man.

"Are you getting hungry?" he asked, and she was glad he didn't press the issue.

"A little." It was after six and up until now, she hadn't thought about food.

"Wait here, I'll be right back."

He rose and entered the kitchen. She heard him rustling around in there, opening the refrigerator door and banging shut the cupboards. The dance of lights in the fireplace mesmerized her for the few minutes he was gone.

Juan Carlos returned with a plate of delicacy cheeses, a bunch of deep red grapes and a loaf of bread. "I hope this will satisfy your hunger. If not, I can cook a few steaks and bake some potatoes."

"No, this is perfect. I don't think I could eat much more."

"Want to sit in front of the fire?"

"Sure." She grabbed a fringy knit throw blanket hanging over the sofa and fanned it out in front of the fireplace. Juan Carlos waited for her to sit, and then handed her the plates before taking his seat facing her.

"This is nice, thank you." She arranged the plates in front of them.

The flickering flames cocooned them in a warm halo of light. She nibbled on the cheese and bread. Miles away from the city, she was at peace in this farmhouse.

She reached for a grape, and met with Juan Carlos's hand as he did the same. Their fingers touched and she lifted her eyes to him. He was staring at her, as if memorizing the way she looked right now. Her heart began to beat faster. Their gazes remained locked for a second, and then she tore a bunch of grapes off and popped one into her mouth.

Outside, breezes blew, making the windows rattle. The distant sound of horses whinnying carried on the wind and she pictured them in their stalls. How long had it been since there was life in those stalls? She hoped the winds wouldn't frighten the animals.

"What is it?" he asked.

"I'm just wondering if the horses are okay out there. The stable walls aren't solid anymore."

"I was going to check on them after you went to bed."

"I'd like to see them."

He pulled air into his lungs and nodded, as if convincing himself of his suggestion. "Then you'll join me."

Juan Carlos held a battery-powered lantern in one hand and Portia's hand in the other. He hadn't planned on spending more time with her tonight. Holding her shaking body and consoling her after the snake incident had stirred a possessive streak in him. He'd wanted to protect her from harm and keep her safe, but having her melt into him, her heartbreaking tears soaking his shirt, had sliced him up inside. He could have held her for hours and not tired of it, yet they'd continued on their search and he'd cursed that damn promise he'd made to her. He'd been desperate to get her to stay on in Alma. And he'd had to agree to her terms with a promise he hoped like hell he could uphold.

Tonight, he'd thought to escape her. Maybe he would have had a drink with Eduardo and Luis or taken a late-night ride, or simply waited until Portia was safely ensconced in her bedroom before making it up to his room. Yet he couldn't refuse Portia her request to join him in the stables.

So here he was, gritting his teeth as she walked beside him under the stars. The stables weren't far and he'd given the bodyguards strict orders to watch without being seen. They were out there somewhere.

The night air had grown cooler, and Portia wrapped both of her arms around herself despite her coat. She might've shivered once or twice.

"Cold?"

"Yes, but I'm okay. I have Scandinavian blood flowing through my veins. Cold weather doesn't bother me."

Juan Carlos hunkered down into his jacket. He'd lived in Miami most of his life. Neither Florida nor Alma got down into freezing temperatures very often. He could tolerate cold weather, but it wasn't his favorite thing. "This is about as cold as it gets here," he said. "At least that's what I'm told."

"It's mostly the wind I don't like."

Right on cue, a howling gust blew from the north. She shivered again and on impulse, he wrapped his free arm over her shoulder and drew her close.

She looked up at him.

"Thanks for keeping me warm," he said.

"Yes, Your Majesty. Anything for the king." A teasing smile played at her lips.

He laughed.

Before long they reached the stables.

"Want me to go in and check for snakes?"

She drew a breath and glanced around the property completely encased in darkness. "I have a feeling it's safer inside than out."

She had a point. There could be all manner of animals roaming the land. Wolves, wild boars and lynx were indigenous to the area. "Okay, then stick close to me."

"You still have your knife?"

"Of course."

"Then you won't be able to shake me."

"I wouldn't even try," he said, quite honestly.

A hum ran through her body. His subtle compliments did crazy things for her ego. After what she'd been through with Miles, that part of her brain had needed nourishment and was now being fed day in and day out by His Hunkiness the King.

She gasped.

"What is it?"

"Oh, nothing. I was just thinking." Jasmine would have a good laugh over this one. Portia was resorting to using terms from a romance novel to describe the handsome, honorable Juan Carlos Salazar II, King of Montoro.

He gripped her hand and led her into the stables. The protective way he held her was another turn-on.

The lantern lit up about five feet of the path in front of them. The place was dank and colder than she'd hoped for the animals. Juan Carlos lifted the lantern to his shoulder and illuminated the stalls. There were shuffling sounds, whinnies and snorts as all four horses came into view. Beauties.

They were curious enough to approach their individual gates. Though she'd been here earlier, Portia could see hints of work done today to make the stable more secure for the horses. The stalls had been shored up, and beds of straw had been laid down. Holes in the walls letting in cold air had been hastily boarded up. Juan Carlos knew how to get things done.

Her eyes darted to the animals' backs. "They're wearing blankets."

"To keep warm. I put Luis on it tonight. They seem comfortable enough, don't they?"

She smiled, relieved. "Yes, I feel better now. They are amazing creatures. Are they yours? I mean do they belong to the palace?"

"We haven't had time to build a remuda of horses for the palace. The transition takes time, but we will have a royal guard on horseback one day soon. These horses belong to me personally, as of two days ago. I have it on good authority they are gentle and trustworthy. I've yet to ride any of them. Tomorrow will be a good test."

"For them or for you?"

His brow arched. "Maybe for all of us."

"Maybe," she agreed. "I've never claimed to be an expert, but I do love animals. What are their names?"

"Come. Let me introduce you." Straw crunched underfoot as they made their way to the first stall. "This is Julio. He's a two-year-old gelding," Juan Carlos said. The sleek charcoal-colored horse had a thick black mane and tail. "He's an Andalusian."

"The horse of kings," she said.

"Yes, I've heard them referred to that way."

"Because they're powerful and sturdy?"

"Because they're intelligent and docile."

She eyed the commanding animal in front of her. He was gorgeous. "Docile?"

"Not as hot-blooded as a thoroughbred. He'll be my mount."

Julio was tall and grand. His curious ink-black eyes watched her. She lifted her hand to him cautiously and he edged closer. She took that as an invitation to stroke the side of his face. "That's it, boy. You and I are going to be good friends," she crooned. Back in Los Angeles, she volunteered at an animal rescue when she wasn't working. Her lifestyle and schedule didn't allow having a pet of her own and she enjoyed donating her time to animals in need.

"You're good with him."

She touched her cheek to Julio's cold nose and he nuzzled her throat eagerly. The force pushed her back a step and she righted herself and giggled. "Oh, he is sweet."

Juan Carlos's gaze touched upon her. Something flickered in his eyes. He swallowed and stroked his hand over his chin. He hadn't shaved today, and his stubble only added to his good looks.

With an inward sigh, she focused back on Julio, giving his mane a solid but loving stroke. She sensed that she had indeed made a new friend today.

Juan Carlos tugged her along to the next stall. "This is Sugar. She's an Arabian. Quick, sharp and good-natured. You'll ride her tomorrow."

"Hello, Sugar. You're a pretty one."

Sugar wasn't as tall or commanding as Julio, but was equally as stately. She had sensitive eyes and seemed friendly. Her chestnut coat glistened under the lantern light. "I'll see you in the morning, girl."

Juan Carlos showed her the other two horses, Arabians named Estrella and Manzana, who were presumably for Eduardo and Luis. Were the king's bodyguards good riders? Was that part of their job description?

New feedbags hung from nails in the walls, replacing the shredded ones from this morning, and a bag of carrots sat on a splintered bench. "Can we give them a treat?"

"Good idea." Juan Carlos went to retrieve the carrots. He dipped his hand inside the bag and came up with four. "One for each."

"Only one?"

"We don't want to spoil them."

"I bet you'd be a tough disciplinarian with your children."

At the mention of children his eyes twinkled and somehow the mischief seemed aimed directly at her. "I'm ready to find out."

Her blood warmed. She hadn't thought along those lines for herself. Parenthood was a long way off for her. But Juan Carlos seemed to know exactly what he wanted. He was resolute, an action taker and at times, he intimated her with his decisiveness. "You want a family one day?"

"Of course...I've lived my life without my parents. I have

no brothers or sisters, although I have my cousins and we have been on good terms. But to have a child of my own, to share that bond with someone I love…it's a dream of mine."

He handed her all four carrots and she walked the stalls, allowing Sugar to nibble at hers first.

"I would think being king would be your dream."

"It's my duty and a role I'm proud to uphold. But a man can have more than one dream, can't he?"

His eyes darkened, his gaze boring into her like a nail being hammered into the wall. He was too close, his expression telling her too much. She couldn't look at him and not see his life all planned out…with her beside him. Were the limited lighting and her silly imagination playing tricks on her?

She turned away from him, taking interest in the horses again. "I suppose." Three beggars were vying for her attention, shuffling their feet, bobbing their heads back and forth. She walked over to Julio next. "Here you go, boy."

Juan Carlos shadowed her to the next two stalls and watched her feed the other Arabians. "Do I make you nervous, Princess?"

Her eyes crinkled as she squeezed them closed. Why did he have to ask her that? She took a breath to steady her nerves and pivoted around. Her back to the stall door, the lie was ready to fall from her lips. Her one eye fluttered, like a wink, but certainly *not* a wink. Oh, boy. She wanted to sink into a black hole. "Y-yes." Damn her honesty. So much for pretending disinterest in him.

Juan Carlos gave her an approving smile as if he'd expected her answer. As if he was pleased with her honesty. "I promised not to pursue you, Portia. But I didn't say I would back off if you came to me. If you decided you wanted me, craved my body as I do yours, I would claim you in an instant and not feel I'd betrayed my vow to you."

He took her hand then, and led her out of the stable. "Come, it's time for bed."

Five

Sugar kept an even pace with Julio as they ambled farther out onto the property. The horse was gentle, took commands well and her sure-footed gait put Portia at ease. She gazed at the cloudless blue sky above. The warmth of the rising sun removed the bite of coolness in the morning air and made the ride pleasant.

Juan Carlos's felt hat shaded his eyes. Portia had put her hat on, too, one that Juan Carlos, who planned for everything, had given her to wear.

"How are you doing?" Juan Carlos asked after five minutes of silence.

"I have no complaints, Your Highness."

He paused. Gosh, why did she goad him? Oh, yeah, to put distance between them. "We've been riding a while now. Is your rear end sore?"

She chuckled. "A little, but I'll survive."

"You just let me know when you want to take a break."

Things had been a little weird between them since last night. Juan Carlos had put a bug in her ear. He'd given her an out. Up until then, her idea to keep their relationship strictly platonic had rested solely on Juan Carlos's shoulders. She'd made him promise to keep his distance. But now he'd tossed the ball into her court. And it had gotten her thinking. But it wasn't a good thing for a woman desperately attracted to a man who was all wrong for her to be given those options.

If you decided you wanted me, craved my body as I do yours...

Those hot words had thrown her. She'd thought of them, of him, all through the night. What would it be like to have Juan Carlos make love to her? What if, here, in this remote, private place, she gave in to temptation and spent the night touching him and being touched. Kissing his perfect mouth, running her cheek along that sexy stubble and nibbling on his throat? What would it be like to have him inside her, the steely velvet of his erection impaling her body?

She squirmed in the saddle, suddenly uncomfortable. Mentally, she forbade Juan Carlos to look over, to see her struggling with thoughts he'd planted inside her head. *Don't look at me. Don't see the expression on my face. Don't see me...wanting you.*

"Portia?"

Darn it. "I'm fine." She stared straight ahead. "Everything's good and dandy."

She sensed him studying her as they rode the length of five football fields until they came upon a graveyard surrounded by a run-down picket fence. The square of ground was full of weeds, unkempt. The neglect was almost sacrilegious. It was out in the middle of nowhere, a place long forgotten.

Juan Carlos slowed his gelding and she did the same. "We'll stop here," he said.

Her rear end rejoiced. She spotted trees that offered perfect shade just yards away. The horses moved toward an oak, massive in size, its roots splayed in all directions.

Juan Carlos dismounted quickly and strode to her. Sugar wasn't as tall as Julio, but Portia still needed help with her dismount. Either that, or run the risk of breaking an ankle when she tried to slide down the horse's left flank.

Juan Carlos's arms were up, reaching for her. She swung her leg over the saddle and his hands found her waist, securing her with a firm grip and guiding her down until her boots hit the ground. He held her for a few beats of time, with her back to his chest, his nose tickling her neck, breathing in her hair. "You smell delicious," he whispered, and then released her.

She sighed. If only she didn't miss his hold on her. Didn't enjoy having him touch her.

I would claim you in an instant and not feel I'd betrayed my vow to you.

He stood beside Julio, gazing at the graveyard as he unlatched a saddlebag and came up with a bottle of water. He walked over to her. "Here," he said. "Take a drink, you must be thirsty."

The water, cool and refreshing, slid down her throat. "That's good." She handed it back to him. His mouth clamped around the lip of the bottle and he tipped it back. He swallowed a big gulp, then another. A trickle of sweat ran down his forehead and he wiped it away.

Simple gestures. Yet her heart raced being near him, sharing water, doing natural things that seemed to bind them together.

"I'd like to check out the graveyard. You can stay here and rest. I'll put a blanket down. You'll be in the shade."

She shook her head. She was curious about the graveyard, too. "I'll come with you."

He nodded and began walking. She followed behind. Wind kicked up and almost blew her hat off. She grabbed it just in time and held it to her head as she approached a wooden gate. Overhead, tree branches made a makeshift archway, and scrolled in wood a sign read: Montoro Family Cemetery.

"So this is where the farm families ended up," she said.

Juan Carlos nodded. "They were probably distant cousins, relatives of my uncles. I'd bet Tantaberra made sure no one has ever come to honor their graves."

They walked through the battered gate. There were many headstones, maybe twenty-five in all. Portia stopped beside Juan Carlos as he bent his head in prayer over one after another. She sent up her own prayers for the lives forgotten here, stepping from one grave site to the next. "Do you know any of these names?" she asked.

"Some sound familiar," he said. The first and middle initials were etched on the headstones along with the last names. "Montoro, of course, and Olivio I've heard mentioned, but many I don't know. I will have this cemetery restored to honor their graves."

Juan Carlos insisted on clearing away the larger of the weeds that had overgrown the area. She bent to help him. "No, please. Your hands will be cut," he said.

"I'll be careful. I want to help." Her chin up, she was ready to do him battle.

He stared at her. "I forgot to bring you gloves." And then he warned, "See that you are careful, Princess."

She smiled and something tugged at her heart. He was angry with himself for the oversight. "I promise to be careful."

He began to pull away tumbleweeds clustered around the graves, staring at the names embedded on the stones as if embedding them into his brain. She, too, had little family. She could see the sadness and the loss in the contoured planes of his face, in the shadows of his dark eyes. The dictatorship had taken so much from his family.

"Let me see your hands," he said when they were all through. They'd cleared away as much as they possibly could. The wind was howling; breezes that had cooled the day's heat were swirling more rapidly now.

She turned her palms up.

Juan Carlos inspected her hands carefully, turning them one way then another.

"See. I'm not a wimpy princess."

He laughed, the shine returning to his eyes. "I'd never describe you that way. I'm grateful for your help."

"You're welcome. But there's one more thing to do."

His right eyebrow shot up. "What would that be?"

"I'll be right back. Don't follow me. I'll only be ten minutes."

She left him in the graveyard. This was something she wanted to do by herself. For his family. He leaned against the post outside the cemetery and watched her march into the fields. Every time she turned, his gaze was glued to her. He wouldn't let her out of his sight. She got that. He was a protector by nature. Gallant. He didn't interfere with her independence though and she appreciated that.

Ten minutes later, she returned to the Montoro family cemetery. Juan Carlos smiled broadly as he gazed at the large bunch of wildflowers she'd gathered in her hands. Some were probably classified as weeds, but they were indisputably pretty anyway. Bluebonnet blues, pale yellows, creamy whites and carnation pinks.

"Would you like to help me lay these down?"

He nodded, a play of deep emotion on his face.

They walked through the cemetery one last time, offering up the flowers to grave sites and headstones to tell the deceased that someone remembered them. Someone cared.

They left the place quietly, Juan Carlos taking her hand. It was a solemn moment, but a sweet one, too. Portia was moved by the care he'd taken with his distant relatives, the honor he'd bestowed upon them.

How many would have just ridden past? How many wouldn't have bothered to stop and clear up the neglect and mess?

This feeling she had for Juan Carlos wasn't going away. It grew stronger each moment she spent in his company.

The horses whinnied upon their return, huffing breaths and stomping hooves. Juan Carlos dipped into the saddlebag again, this time to offer the animals a handful of oats to keep them satisfied. "There, now. You two be quiet. No more complaining." He stroked Julio's head a few times and then turned to Portia. "Let's sit a minute. Take a rest."

"All right."

He grabbed a blanket and spread it out under the tree. The shade was no longer an issue; the weather had cooled and gray clouds were gathering in the skies. She shivered and walked to her saddlebag, picking out a jacket from the things she'd brought along.

"Cold?"

"A little bit."

"We can head back."

It was too early to return to the house. They had more ground to cover and she didn't want to delay their mission because of a little cold weather. Her family hailed from Scandinavia, where food was put out on windowsills to freeze quickly, where the elderly lived over one hundred years because germs couldn't survive the environment. She refused to slow Juan Carlos down.

"Ten minutes is all I need," she said.

She put on the jacket and sat down. He sat next to her and roped his arm around her. It seemed only natural to put her head on his shoulder.

"There is a giant rock formation about half an hour from here. The terrain is rough but these horses can make it up there. I found it on a GPS map of the area." His voice soothed her even as he spoke of a tough task. She closed her eyes. "I think it's a good hiding place for the artwork. I suspect caves have formed between the interlocking rocks. At least, that's what I'm hoping."

"Sounds reasonable. We'll check it out."

"Are you up for it? We can return tomorrow if you're not."

"I'm up for it," she said. "We're already halfway there, aren't we?"

"Yes, but the weather might be a problem."

"It won't be, Juan Carlos. I'm not a wimpy princess, remember?"

Laughter rumbled from his chest. "How can I forget? You keep reminding me."

"Good," she said, snuggling deeper into his arms.

The solid beats of his heart were like the revving of a powerful engine. It was dangerous and thrilling and though she hated to move, it was time to break this cozy moment with him. She slid away from his grip and rose to her feet. "I'm ready when you are."

He bounded up, regret in his eyes, as if she'd taken something precious from him.

From both of them.

The rocks were adobe-red, huge and intimidating. They were also beautiful against the landscape of gray skies and brown earth. The horses treaded with agility through the gravelly terrain, their sure-footed gait assuring her she would not fall to her death as they climbed a plateau that led to the face of the mountain. "This is amazing. It reminds me of Sedona back in the States. Have you ever been there?"

"In Arizona?" Juan Carlos gave his head a shake. "No, but I've seen pictures. It's an artist colony, isn't it?"

"Yes, among other things. There are some wonderful galleries and art exhibits in the area. I studied there one summer."

"Did you ever climb the rocks?"

She nibbled her lower lip. "I'd been tempted a few times, but no, I didn't climb the rocks. I was there for the art. Are we climbing rocks today?" she asked pointedly.

Juan Carlos spread his gaze over the entire mountainside, studying the terrain. "Just like back then, you came here for the art. So no. We don't have to climb the rocks.

The openings seem to be on the lower levels. We can reach them without climbing."

She released a tight breath. She didn't like heights and they didn't like her, so no rock climbing was a good thing. "I'm excited. I have a good feeling about this," she said. "I'm imagining the artwork tucked inside the mountain somewhere, deep inside a cave."

"Then let's go find it," he said.

He dismounted and strode over, lifting his hands to her waist again. Dust kicked up by the strong wind mingled with the potent scent of horseflesh and earth. More threatening clouds gathered above, and a shiver shook her shoulders as she slid into his arms. His hands steadied her until her boots hit the ground. Then he took the reins of both horses and they began walking toward a row of rocks, stacked neatly like building blocks five stories high.

He stopped at the base of a formation where two giant boulders separated and an opening appeared. It wasn't much wider than a double-door refrigerator, but large enough to allow a man to enter. "Wait here," he said. "Stay with the horses. I'll go inside and see if it goes anywhere. It might be a dead end. I'll be back in a minute." He pulled out a flashlight and turned to her. "Okay?"

She took the reins with one hand and stroked Sugar's nose with the other. Eyeing him, Portia confessed, "I'm not very patient."

A grin crossed his features, that gorgeous mouth of his lifting crookedly. "Good to know."

For real? The man had a one-track mind. "Come and get me, if you find anything."

"Will do. We're in this together," he said, and then disappeared into the gap.

Just then, the wind knocked her back against the rocks. It was fierce today. She huddled behind the horses, allowing them to block the sharp bite of cold. Her teeth chattered anyway. Goodness, it seemed as if Juan Carlos had already been gone for hours but it was more like a minute or two.

Then she heard his approach, his footfalls scraping the ground of the cave. Thank God. A thrill shimmied through her belly. She really wasn't patient, not when it came to this. If only they could find the artwork today.

When he emerged from the opening, she took one look at Juan Carlos's expression and her shoulders slumped. "You didn't find it?"

He shook his head. "Not in there." His eyes were solemn as they toured over her face and body. "You're freezing."

"I'm...not."

His lips twisted at her denial. Then he turned away from her and grappled with both of their saddlebags, freeing them from their fasteners and tossing them over his shoulder. "Come," he said, handing her their blankets. "It's warmer inside. Besides, there is something I want to show you."

"Really? What is it?"

"You'll see." He took her frigid hand and immediately the blood began pulsing more warmly through her veins. One would think he was a flaming hot furnace with how easily his touch could heat her up through and through.

He led her into the darkness. The flashlight illuminated the way and she squinted as her eyes adjusted. Around her, stone walls made up a cavelike space, tall enough for them to stand in and wide enough for an entire hunting party to take refuge. The air inside was cool, but without the outside wind gusts it was warmer by a dozen degrees. "You're right, it is warmer in here."

"Take a look at this," he said, aiming his flashlight at a far corner.

Eyes appeared first, round and frightened, and then the light followed the length of the animal, stretched out on the ground nursing her young. "Kittens!"

Five tiny bodies fought for a place at mama's table, eager for their meal. The mother cat, striped in reds, browns and grays, eyed both Juan Carlos and Portia warily. "She's scared," Portia said. "Poor mama." She'd had lots of experience with birthing pups and kittens at the rescue where she volunteered. "She might be feral, though I doubt it. She would've been hissing and scratching her way out of here by now. The babies look to be only a few weeks old."

"You think she's domestic?" he asked.

Portia crouched down, studying the cat from five feet away. "I think she's somewhere in between. She might've been abandoned. She's doing what comes natural and found this place to have her kittens. Cats like dark cool isolated places to give birth."

"Well, she found that," Juan Carlos said, keeping his voice soft. Both of them whispered now, so as not to startle the wary cat.

"I wonder if she's hungry. She looks pretty scrawny."

"About all we've got is water and sandwiches."

"Water, for sure. She'll need that. And we can pull out cheese and bits of meat from our sandwiches. If she's hungry enough, she'll eat it."

"Good idea. I'm getting hungry. Maybe we should stay inside and eat, too."

Portia kept her eyes fixed on the new little family. "I'd like that."

Outside the wind howled. The refuge they'd found would do for now until the weather let up. Portia worked with Juan Carlos to fix the mama cat a meal of beef and cheese, and laid it out on a cloth napkin. She was at a loss as to where to put the water. They had narrow-necked bottles and not much else that would work for a bowl.

"Here," Juan Carlos said, handing her his hat, tipped upside down in his palm. "She needs it more than I do."

Under the dim flashlight rays, his eyes were full of

compassion. He was a problem solver, but it was more than that. He was doing this as much for Portia's sake as he was for the sweet cat family. "You'll freeze your head off when we go back out there."

"Not if we stay here overnight."

Her heart skipped. To be alone with Juan Carlos all night? She couldn't possibly. He didn't mean it. It was hard enough knowing he was sleeping down the hallway at the farmhouse. "Surely, we can't."

His eyes twinkled. "It was a nice thought, though. Being trapped in here with you all night…*to watch over the kittens*."

Blood rushed to her cheeks. Suddenly, the cold dank cave sizzled with heat. She coughed, to cover errant thoughts of spending the night with Juan Carlos, of wearing nothing but a blanket to keep each other warm. His arms would wrap around her, and then their bare bodies would conform, mesh and he would nudge himself inside her.

"Are you okay, sweetheart?"

He knew. The sparkle in his eyes lit up even brighter.

"I'm fine."

"Are you sure?"

"Perfectly," she snapped. Goodness, she sounded like a witch.

He shrugged a shoulder, a smile teasing his lips as he handed her the cat's meal. "Do you want to take it to her?"

She nodded, recovering from the image that had sprung up in her head. "I'll try. I hope she doesn't run."

Portia took pained steps toward the cat, catching her eye and hoping her slow movements would show her she wasn't a threat. The cat's tail tensed and arched, her head came up and those tigerlike eyes watched her every move. Then she meowed.

"It's okay, sweet mama. I don't want to hurt you. Look, I have food. I hope you'll eat it."

The cat hissed, but she was just protecting her young. "This is as far as I'll go," Portia said softly. "See." She set down the napkin two feet from her and as soon as she backed away, the cat sniffed at it. "Put the hat down carefully," she said to Juan Carlos. He was only half a step behind and he set the water down next to the food. Then his hand clamped over her arm as he guided her several feet back, the beam of light dimming on the mama cat.

"Chances are, she won't eat or drink anything until she gives everything a complete smell test."

"We've done what we could for them," Juan Carlos said. "They are cute."

"Adorable," Portia said. The fuzzy fur babies were nestled against mama cat's underside, many of them satisfied and ready to nap.

Juan Carlos spread the blanket out and they began eating their sandwiches. Nibbling on her sliced steak sandwich sitting cross-legged, her eyes kept darting over to the cats.

"She'll eat eventually," Juan Carlos said.

"She's starving, but she won't make a move until we leave."

"Then we'll go as soon as we finish up here."

She nodded and within a few minutes, Portia was back atop Sugar, waiting for Juan Carlos to take his mount. She was torn about leaving the kittens in there, hoping the mama would survive the cold and be able to care for her young babes. How would she feed herself after the food they left behind was gone?

"Where to next?" Portia asked, blinking away tears, trying to distract herself from the sick feeling in her gut. She was a softie when it came to animals.

He stared into her eyes and smiled. "They'll survive. Don't worry."

He'd read her mind, but unlike most people, Portia didn't believe cats had nine lives. Sometimes, they couldn't beat the odds. If only this wasn't one of those times. She mustered a smile, but her heart wasn't in it.

"Since the wind has died down, I'd like to check out two of the nearby dwellings while we're here. If you stay put, I'll go in and be out quickly." He pointed north. "They aren't far. We'll get home before we lose light."

"I'm fine with that." She really was, though part of her wanted to stay behind and nurture the kittens. But that was impossible. Mama cat wanted no part of them right now. "I like the plan."

He nodded. "Let's go."

After showering and getting dressed, Portia marched downstairs in new jeans and a beige ribbed sweater to start dinner. She wasn't going to have Juan Carlos waiting on her. She planned to do her part. As she reached the bottom stair, she saw the fire crackling in the hearth and warmth settled around her. It was after seven; the darkened sky was lit with a scant few stars tonight. Her stomach grumbled, protesting over only having a light afternoon lunch. Thank God Juan Carlos wasn't around to hear the commotion her belly made.

The blaze in the front room beckoned. She could just as easily plop in a chair and watch the flickering fire, but she moved on and headed for the kitchen.

She found fresh tomatoes, whole garlic cloves, cans of tomato paste and packaged pasta in the cupboard. "Spaghetti it is." She wasn't a bad cook. She could crush tomatoes with the best of them.

Inside the fridge, she also found a covered dish of already cooked meatballs.

It seemed as though Juan Carlos had kitchen minions.

She wasn't complaining.

She turned the stove on, grabbed a cast-iron pan, peeled and mashed two garlic cloves with a butcher knife and poured a little oil in the pan. Garlicky steam billowed up and pungent scents filled the room.

The back door opened and Juan Carlos walked in. "Mmm. Smells great in here."

"I hope you like spaghetti and meatballs."

"Who doesn't?" he said, coming to stand beside her.

"Hand me those tomatoes," she said, fully aware of his freshly groomed presence beside her.

Instead of walking to get them, he grabbed her waist with one hand from behind and stretched the other hand out as far as he could, snapping up three ripe tomatoes from the counter without leaving her side. "Here you go."

His touch sent heat spiraling through her body. "Into the pot with them, please."

"Like this?" He lowered them down gently, his face brushing against her hair.

He was a tease.

"Thank you."

"Don't you have to peel them?"

She shook her head. "The skin will peel off easily later from the heat. And then, you'll get to crush them."

"Me?"

"Yes, you. They need a manly crush."

"Well then, I'm your man."

She stopped and gazed into his eyes. Those words. They could be true. If she allowed it. Juan Carlos had owned up to his deal. He hadn't really come on to her, but every single second of every single minute of the day, he told her in his own silent, heart-melting way that he wanted her.

"Yes, well, uh…just let me get the meatballs."

How was that for a change of subject?

"I can crush those, too," he said.

She laughed. "I'm sure you can."

Dinner was half an hour later. They decided to eat in the kitchen this time, at a wooden table with inlaid painted

tiles. One of the nearby windows faced the backyard garden, now bathed in starlight, and if she squinted she could
see the plants. It was cozy and nice, and she'd put out a
mason jar candle that cast a pretty glow over the room.
Juan Carlos kept glancing at his watch as they forked spaghetti into their mouths and spoke of easy simple things.
She refused to think any more about the snake with the
severed head lying in that shack. Or the cemetery with so
many families who'd lived here before.

After his eyes shifted to his watch once again, her curiosity got the better of her. "Am I keeping you from something?"

There was no television in the house. No important soccer games to watch. No distractions. Maybe he couldn't
wait to get upstairs to finish the book he'd been reading.

He shook his head. "There's no place I'd rather be than
right here."

Oh, she'd stepped into that one.

"The meal is delicious," he said.

"It was all that manly crushing," she remarked, and he
put his fork down to grin at her.

She jingled in places that normally jangled. He turned
her life upside down. She'd miss him when this adventure
was over and she went back to LA.

She rose and grabbed up their empty plates. "Would
you like another helping?"

He patted his flat, washboard stomach. "No, I'd better stop here."

"Then no cherry cobbler? It seems the kitchen minions
made a trip to the bakery."

"Maybe later, Princess."

She washed dishes and he dried. It was all so domestic.
Well, as domestic as she'd seen on the Hallmark Chan-
nel. Her life was hardly a typical American tale. What

did one do after the dishes were cleaned and the night loomed ahead?

Her gaze slid to Juan Carlos, wiping his hands on a kitchen towel. He folded the towel neatly, set it on the counter and smoothed it out. With a slight tilt of his head, he sought her out, a question on his lips.

Before he could voice his thoughts, the purr of an engine reached her ears. Juan Carlos strode to the kitchen window that faced the side yard. "It's Eduardo. He ran an errand for me. Wait here, I'll be right back."

"Why?"

But he dashed out the door before giving her an answer.

She heard their voices and strained to hear what they were saying, but she couldn't make it out.

The back door opened with the slight kick of Juan Carlos's boot and he strode in holding a wire cage in both hands.

Meeeow.

The cats! Juan Carlos had the mama cat and her kittens.

Eduardo followed behind him, his hair rumpled, drops of blood staining his scratched hands. He looked almost as frazzled as the cat.

"Eduardo, you're bleeding!"

"Hazard of the job," he mumbled.

It took only a second for her to figure out what he'd done. What they'd both done. Juan Carlos had sent Eduardo on a mission to rescue mama cat and her babies.

"He wouldn't let me go," Juan Carlos was saying.

"My job is to protect you, Your Majesty."

"Not from cats." The king appeared annoyed at himself for allowing Eduardo to do the job he'd wanted to do. "I should've gone. Now look at you."

"Better me than you. They're nothing but a few scrapes. She put up a good fight." Eduardo grinned. "She is a feisty one."

Juan Carlos gritted his teeth. "Those injuries should've been on my hands."

"Stop arguing, you two," Portia said. "What you both did was very kind. Juan Carlos, take the cats in the living area. The room is dark and cozy. It might put mama at ease. Eduardo, come with me. I'll take care of your hands." She marched into the bathroom and heard footsteps behind her. Grateful that Eduardo had obeyed her order, she grabbed a washrag, filled a bowl of warm water and pointed for him to sit on the edge of the bathtub.

Goodness.

She sat, too, and took his big hands in hers, scouring over half a dozen scratch marks. "She must've been very frightened."

"That made two of us."

"Oh, Eduardo." She began dabbing at the wounds. He flinched, but took the pain. She dabbed a little more gently, cleansing and dressing his wounds. "There."

"The king is very angry with me. Luis and I both, we convinced him not to go. He wanted to do this thing… for you."

Portia closed her eyes. "I…know."

Her chest tightened. It was the sweetest gesture anyone had ever done for her. Or tried to do.

"He is a proud man. But don't worry, he won't be angry for long."

"He won't?"

"No. I think not. And thank you, Eduardo, for rescuing the animals."

She placed a chaste kiss on his cheek. He was large, built like a block of stone, but his expression softened and as he rose, he bowed to her with his eyes twinkling.

And she felt as though she'd made a new friend.

Six

"Do you think she'll try to escape if we open the cage?" Portia asked as she sat facing Juan Carlos on the floor beside the fire. The cage was between them. The leery mama cat's eyes were guarded and wide. Portia made a move to get a better look at the babies, and a mewling hiss, one born of fear more than anything else, pressed through the feline's tight lips.

Juan Carlos shrugged. "She has nowhere to go. The house is locked up and the doors to this room are closed. Right now, I think she needs to see us and know we won't harm her."

"I think you're right." Portia tilted her head to one side. "You're intuitive when it comes to animals."

While she had been bandaging up Eduardo, Juan Carlos had set out a bowl of water and a plate of leftover cheese bits for when they let the cat out later.

"At least she won't starve tonight," he said.

Outside the wind was howling again, even pushing through the flue of the fireplace. The flames scattered momentarily in the hearth, blazing wildly before returning to a normal easy burn again. "No, she won't starve and the kittens will thrive. Thanks to you."

He kept his eyes on the fire, not commenting, refusing to take any credit for the deed. It didn't matter. He couldn't hide his intentions from her.

"They're the cutest little things," she said, her voice squeaking. She couldn't help it. Babies in all forms brought her voice to a higher pitch. Who in the world didn't love furry new kittens? "I'm glad they're here."

She had a view of his profile, so sharp and defined. Firelight played across his face and when he turned to her, his expression softened. "Me, too."

"Why didn't you tell me your plan to rescue her?" It was what all his watch-glancing had been about. It made sense to her now and she was incredibly relieved to learn the reason for his impatience. "Was it a surprise?"

He nodded. "I didn't want you to be disappointed if Eduardo couldn't bring her back."

And there it was. On his face. Concern. Caring. Almost love.

Something shifted inside her. It wasn't a blunt move, but something that had been tilting and leaning gradually, like dominoes toppling in super slow motion. She could feel each one fall, until every shred of her defenses was being taken down by this good, kind, *sexy* man.

"It's late," he said.

No, it wasn't.

"We should unlatch the cage now and leave her, so she can eat."

"Okay," Portia said, sorely disappointed. She knew that meant saying good night to Juan Carlos and parting ways at the top of the stairs once again.

He sighed as he rose to his feet and strode to the fireplace to take up a metal poker. He slashed at the logs, until only simmering embers heated the brick floor inside.

Portia carefully unlatched the hook on the cage and flipped it away. The wire door swung open but the cat stayed put. "Here you go, Duchess. You're free now."

"Duchess?" Juan Carlos turned to her.

"She needs a name." She shrugged. "It seems fitting somehow."

He smiled, but his eyes remained hooded. "Duchess it is. What's one more royal around here, anyway? Well, I'll say good-night now. We have an early call tomorrow."

They did. They were going even farther out on the grounds in the Jeep.

"Are you coming up?" he asked. He had almost reached the hallway door.

She rose to her feet and stared at him from across the room. Words wouldn't come. Her heart was thumping, drowning out everything else in her world.

"Portia?"

"What if…?" A swallow stole her next words.

He waited, his face in the shadows so she couldn't see his expression.

"What if I said I was a w-wimpy princess, after all?"

He paused. "Would you rather not go out in the Jeep tomorrow?"

"No." She shook her head, her hair falling like a sheet around her shoulders. "Juan Carlos, it means I don't want you to go to bed…"

He stepped out of the shadows, his eyes dark, intense. Waiting.

She froze. Oh, God, she was breaking every rule she'd ever committed to.

"Say it."

The force of his command sent thrills careening through her body.

"Say it, Portia."

He wouldn't break his vow to her. She had to do it. He'd told her as much just the other day. His honor meant that much to him and he wouldn't have it any other way.

"Without me." She nodded, convincing herself. "I don't want you to go to bed without—"

And suddenly, he was there in front her, gazing into her eyes, cupping her head in his hands and brushing his lips over hers. Once. Twice. His hungry mouth devoured her over and over again. His arms wrapped around her, his hand brushing away her hair tenderly, his body trembling as he took her in kiss after kiss.

She was lost in the goodness of him, the thrill of his hands finally on her. The scent of his skin. The power of his body. Tears spilled down her cheeks at the clarity of this moment. She was his. He was hers. It was so easy, so simple. How had she managed to keep this amazing man at bay? How had she not realized earlier how perfect they would be for each other?

"Portia, don't cry," he was murmuring between kisses.

"I'm…happy, Juan Carlos."

"Oh, God. How I've waited for this. For *you*. Say my name again."

"Juan Carlos. Juan Carlos. Juan Carlos."

He grinned, a flash of white teeth in a broad happy smile that branded her heart. His gaze roved over her face and traveled the length of her body, his smile fading into something delicious. Something dangerous. And something she no longer feared. His eyes burned with want, the heat in them back full force. The man knew how to smolder.

"Portia." He breathed her name as if his life depended on it. "I need you."

"I need you, too," she admitted softly. She reached for the hem of his shirt, pushing the material up his torso.

"No," he said, taking her hands in his. "We'll do this right."

And in the next instant, he swooped her up into his arms. She wound her arms around his neck and as he headed upstairs, she pressed her lips to his, kissing him until they reached the threshold to his room.

"Here we are," he said, his voice reverent, as if the next step he took would be monumental. He carried her over the threshold with great ceremony and smiled at her. "I've wanted you since the moment I laid eyes on you."

"You have me," she said softly.

"God. I cannot wait much longer, but I will not rush with you." He lowered her down onto the bed. The mattress cushioned her body and then his hands were there, removing her sweater and unbuttoning her blouse, spreading it out so he could see her breasts. "You are beautiful," he said, planting both hands on the mattress beside her head, trapping her. She may never want to escape. His kiss was rough and hungry, and when she looked up, the sharp lines of his face tightened, a passionate preamble of what was to come. Her skin prickled in anticipation.

His fingertips grazed over her breasts lightly, hovering, teasing the sensitive tips. Hot liquid warmth pooled between her thighs. Then he wound his hands behind her back and she lifted herself up enough for him to unfasten her bra. With his help, she shrugged out of it and then lay back down.

"Fair is fair," he said, rising to grab the hem of his shirt. He pulled it up and over his head. Her mouth gaped open and she took a hard swallow, gazing at the tempting sculpted bronze chest.

"That is totally *unfair*," she whispered.

A smile spread across his face as he bent on his knees to remove her boots, her belt and then slowly, achingly moved the zipper of her pants down. Cool air hit her thighs, but she was too swamped already, too raggedly consumed by heat for that to have any lasting effect. He tugged at one pant leg and then the other, until she was free of them. All that was left on her body was a pair of teeny hot pink panties. "I like your style, Princess," he murmured, sliding up her thighs to hook the hem with his fingers.

"I like yours." She gulped.

He smiled again and dragged her panties down her legs.

Then the mattress dipped as he lowered down next to her. Immediately, his scent wafted to her nose: fresh soap and a hint of lime. She squeezed her eyes closed, breathing him in. He cupped her head and kissed her lips, her chin, her throat. "Let me explore you, Portia," he whispered.

She nodded. "If I can explore you."

"Be my guest," he said, his tone once again reverent. He fell back against the bed.

She rose up part of the way to lay a hand on his chest. Heat sizzled under her palm as she slid her fingers over tight skin and muscle. His chest was a work of art and as she continued to explore, he took sharp gasps of breath. Empowered now, she moved more confidently, her fingers flat over his nipples, weaving them through tiny chest hairs and reaching his broad shoulders. She nibbled on him there, nipping his hot skin and breathing the scent of raw sex emanating from his pores. "You are amazing, Juan Carlos," she said. And suddenly she was eager for him to explore her, to touch her in ways she'd secretly dreamed about. "Your turn."

She lay back on the bed and he rose over her to take a leisurely tour of her naked body, his eyes a beacon of light flowing over every inch of her. Then his hands began to trace the contours of her body, caressing her curves and moving effortlessly over her skin. He was thorough, leaving no part of her untouched. Goose bumps rose on her arms and legs, his precision and utmost sensitivity leaving her trembling in his wake.

Next, he covered her trembling body with his, wrapping her in his heat and claiming her with his presence. She bore his weight and peered up at him. He was amazing, so handsome, so incredibly virile. His hands cushioned her breasts, massaging them until the peaks were two sensitive tips. The pads of his thumbs flicked at them gently, and something powerful began to build and throb below her waist.

She had not been with a man in a long time. It felt so good. So right. Being with him.

He pressed her a little harder and she cried out. "Juan Carlos."

It seemed to satisfy him. He took her in an earth-shattering kiss, pressing her mouth open and sweeping into her. She moved under him, arching her hips, that feeling below her waist becoming stronger and stronger the longer the kiss went on.

His hand was moving again, leaving her full breasts and moving down her torso, past her navel and below her waist, where she ached and ached for him. "Trust me," he said.

All she could do was nod.

And his hands and mouth worked magic on her, shredding her into tiny pieces, squeezing tortured moans from her lips and making her squirm until she finally reached a fantastic, bone-melting orgasm.

"Juan Carlos," she breathed, lifting her head to find his eyes on her as he unbuckled his belt. He shucked out of his clothes quickly and sheathed himself, in all his naked glory, with a condom.

He touched her where she was most sensitive, lending her comfort and warmth in the aftermath of her pulsing release. She relaxed and eased back slowly, as another fire began to build. "I've waited for you all of my life, Portia. And now, you're mine."

She was ready for him when he entered her, wanting him this way, taking his weight and watching a fiery veil of passion burn in his eyes. He began to rock back and forth, each thrust a love note, a daring caress and sugary candy for her hungry body. "You are all I will ever need," he murmured.

She smiled as he pressed farther and farther inside her body. She was his. *He* was all she would ever need and as she met his driving rhythm, arching up and down, her breaths heavy, her body primed, she found solace and peace in his arms and lust and desire in his bed.

Juan Carlos drew a deep breath into his lungs. He'd often dreamed of waking up next to Portia, and now his very fantasy had come true. He turned his head and watched her chest rise and fall slowly. Her hair fanned across the pillow. He ached to touch it and sift the strands through his fingers. He wanted to kiss her awake and then make love to her again. But the sun had barely risen and the day would prove a long one. She needed her sleep. He'd worn her out last night. He shook his head at the thoughts running through his mind. He couldn't touch her again this morning and have her think he was lecherous, waking her with only one thing on his mind.

He smiled. He would come to her again sometime today. It would be hard to keep to the task at hand, but they were on a mission. Though a wicked part of him wanted to play hooky today. Why couldn't they just stay in bed all day? The States had snow days. Why couldn't he declare a Royal Day?

A little noise pressed through her lips, a moan that he'd come to know. Last night, she'd moaned plenty and turned his world on end.

She shifted toward him and one hand—warm, delicate and soft—flopped onto his cheek. He moved his head enough to press his lips there and kiss her.

"Hi," she said, smiling, though her eyes were still closed.

"Good morning, sweetheart."

"Is it time to get up?"

"You can stay in bed as long as you'd like."

"With you?"

"Yes, only with me."

Her eyes opened and he gazed into their sleep-hooded amazing blue depths. He could fall into those eyes and never want to return.

"Juan Carlos," she said, "last night was…"

"I know."

"I didn't know it could be that good."

He leaned in and kissed her tenderly. "I'm humbled to hear you say that."

"Humbled? Not over-the-moon, cocky and feeling proud of yourself?"

He chuckled. "Maybe that, too."

"I had…uh, you know. Three times. That's never happened before."

"Keep telling me things like that and we'll never get out of this bed."

She grinned and reached over to move a tendril of hair off his forehead, her delicate fingertips sliding down his cheek. He loved it when she touched him. "You know, that doesn't sound like a bad idea."

He caught her wrist and kissed her pulse point. "We can make that happen, sweetheart."

"If only," she said, sighing, her head falling back against the pillow. "But we need to finish what we started."

She would be leaving soon. She didn't have to say the words. He had only a few more days with her, before she would head back to the States. How quickly reality reared its ugly head. "We will finish it, one way or another."

"I hope we find something today," she said.

"We'll give it a good shot."

"I should get dressed. I'm anxious to see how our little family is doing."

She meant the cats. Juan Carlos had almost forgotten about them. "Right. Let's go check on them together."

She rose from the bed and turned away. As she fitted

her arms through the sleeves of his shirt, he glimpsed her lush blond hair falling down her back, the creamy texture of her skin, her rounded backside and the coltlike legs that had wrapped around him last night.

He sighed, enjoying the view and ignoring his body's immediate reaction to her. He threw on a pair of jeans and a T-shirt. Hand in hand, they strolled out of the bedroom and into the living area.

"Shhh," she said, spying the cat nursing her kittens outside the cage on a loop rug in front of the fireplace. "We don't want to startle her."

Duchess was resting with her head down, her eyes closed, allowing her five offspring to take their morning meal. Juan Carlos was moved by the sweet look on Portia's face as she silently watched mama and babies. He wrapped his arm around her shoulder and drew her closer, kissing the top of her head. How could he ever let this woman go? The answer was simple: he couldn't. It wouldn't be easy but he would convince her to stay. And marry him.

"Do you think Duchess will eat eggs?" she asked Juan Carlos as she scrambled four eggs in a cast-iron skillet. Morning sunshine brightened the kitchen, filling it with warmth. Bacon sizzled on the griddle and toast was cooking under the broiler. "I'll put a little cheese on them."

"You can try," he said, pouring two mugs of coffee. "She'll eat when she gets hungry enough. I'll send Eduardo out this morning for cat food."

She'd managed to get fresh water over to the cat without her running for cover. Duchess was still wary, but the kittens slowed her down or else she probably would've bolted when Portia set the bowl down. In time, Duchess would come to trust her. Sadly, she wouldn't be around long enough to see it.

She had work waiting for her in Los Angeles.

It was for the best that she leave Alma. She couldn't fall in love with Juan Carlos. He didn't fit into her plans for a quiet, unassuming life. Yet spending time with him had been magnificent.

He came up behind her, kissed the side of her throat and ran a hand up her thigh. She tensed in all the good places. He'd asked her not to dress yet, and now she knew why. She was only wearing his shirt, which gave him easy access to her body. Not that she minded. Heavens, no. She loved him touching her. "I'll be right back," he said. "Coffee's ready and on the table."

"Where are you going?" she asked.

"Don't be so nosy. I'll be back before you know it."

She smiled and turned, and his arms automatically wound around her. "See that you are. Breakfast is almost ready."

"Bossy, Princess," he said, staring at her mouth.

Her heart skipped a beat and a moment passed between them before he kissed the tip of her nose.

She shrugged a shoulder. "Kings."

He laughed and exited the back door.

Juan Carlos may have originally been a reluctant king, but there was no doubt in her mind that he was good for Alma and that he would put the country's welfare above all else. As it should be. Alma had been through tough times under a ruthless dictatorship. The country needed a strong man.

So do you.

No, she couldn't go there. The map was already drawn up for both of them, and after this little interlude, their paths wouldn't cross again.

After she set the table, Juan Carlos returned holding a bouquet of tall azure flowers. "For you," he said, handing her all but one stem. "Scilla hispanica."

"They're beautiful." She lifted them to her nose. "Are these from the garden?"

He nodded. "Spanish bluebells. They're almost a perfect match to your eyes, sweetheart." He pinched off the end of the one he still held and fitted it behind her right ear. "There. Now you're perfect."

"Hardly," she said.

"I think so."

"You think I'm bossy."

"Dressed like that, cooking my breakfast and wearing flowers in your hair? I can deal with a little bossiness."

She shook her head. "You're wicked." And so very thoughtful.

"So I'm told."

He took the flowers from her hands, snapped off the tips of the stems and arranged the bouquet in an old thick green glass bottle. After he filled it with water, he placed it on the table. "Have a seat, Princess," he said, pulling out a chair. "I'll serve you."

She had a protest on her lips, but Juan Carlos's expression wouldn't allow arguing. "Yes, Your Highness."

He smiled. "Good. I'm glad you know who the real boss is around here."

Portia's heart swelled. And as they sat down and ate, easy conversation flowed between them. Juan Carlos touched her hand often, as if needing the connection. She leaned over to brush hair from his forehead and he'd steal a kiss or two. They were in sync with each other; nothing had ever been as perfect as it was now, with the two of them doing ordinary everyday things, like cooking breakfast, sharing a meal and worrying over the cat family.

"So what will happen to Duchess and her babies when we have to leave here?" she asked.

"She'll become the official palace cat, of course."

"And the kittens?"

"We'll find them good homes, Portia. Don't worry."

Her eye twitched. "I know you're doing this for me." She covered his hand with hers. "Thank you."

The feelings between them were getting too heavy, too fast. She had no way of stopping it, short of leaving him right here and now. But she couldn't do that. Not only did she not want to, but she'd promised to spend a few days here helping with the search, and with the exception of a snake decapitation, she was having a wonderful time.

"You're welcome. Now, if you'll excuse me, I have to speak with Luis about a few matters."

Juan Carlos rose and began clearing the dishes. What a guy. She bounded up quickly and took the plates from his hands. "I'll take care of that," she said with enough authority to keep prison inmates in line.

"Okay," he said. "Thanks."

He bent his head and took her in a long amazing kiss. When their lips parted and he was through, her head spun. "That was…promising."

He grinned, shaking his head at her understatement. "Get ready. We'll be leaving in a little while. Unless you've changed your mind and want to play hooky today."

He was reaching inside her shirt. She slapped his hand away and pointed. "Go."

He went.

And Portia cleared the dishes and cleaned up the kitchen. She checked on Duchess and her brood; they were all sleeping. What a pretty serene picture they made, a mass of calico colors and balls of fluff all nestled together. She was grateful they'd have a home after they left the farmhouse. Her heart had never been so full.

Thirty minutes later, Portia climbed into the passenger side of the Jeep and Juan Carlos got behind the wheel. They said goodbye to Luis, though that didn't mean anything. He was sure to follow. Eduardo had gone into the local town on a cat food mission.

"All set?" Juan Carlos said, gunning the motor. "Strapped in?"

She nodded. The weather was glorious, the temperature in the mid-seventies with clear blue skies. She wore a lightweight white jacket that billowed in the breeze as Juan Carlos drove off and picked up speed.

"We're going out about five miles," he shouted over the engine's roar.

She sat back and relaxed, enjoying the scenery, excitement stirring her bones. Maybe today they'd find the art treasures.

For four hours they traveled at a snail's pace over lush lands, where wildflowers and lantana grew in abundance, the vista opening up to a prairie as they scoured the grounds looking for possible hiding places. They came upon another shack but after a thorough inspection, with Juan Carlos insisting on going inside first, they found absolutely nothing. Not even a snake.

"We have a little more land to cover before we head back," Juan Carlos said, and she heard the disappointment in his voice. She, too, was disappointed.

"Let's stop for lunch by that little lake we passed a few minutes ago." Maybe regrouping would give them a fresh perspective.

"It wasn't much of a lake," Juan Carlos said. "More like an oversize pond."

She entwined their fingers. "But it's pretty there and I'm getting hungry."

He smiled and gave her hand a squeeze. That was all it took for her heart to do a little flip. "Okay, we'll have a picnic." And he maneuvered the Jeep around, heading for the lake.

Warm breezes ruffled her hair and sweat beaded her

forehead as the sun climbed high overhead. She loved being outdoors. Much of her time in the States was spent indoors at art exhibits, galleries or simply poring over books and surfing the internet. She took a full breath of Alma air and vowed not to let disappointment ruin their day.

They'd packed a lunch and had a blanket. That was all they would need.

Juan Carlos braked the Jeep several yards from the water's edge. There were no shade trees so they used the vehicle to provide a bit of cover. From Luis. They were always being watched, but Portia was starting to get used to the idea and it wasn't as creepy as she'd once thought. Juan Carlos jumped down first as she gathered up the blanket. Then he reached for her and helped her down, crushing her body against his and taking her in a long, slow, deliberate kiss.

When he released her, her breathing sped up, coming in short clips. The blanket between them was her only salvation from being ravaged on the spot. She clung to it and backed away. "I should spread this out."

He backed off, too. "You do that," he said, his voice tight. "I'll get the cooler."

Once everything was in place, they sat down facing the water, their backs propped against the side of the Jeep. "The kitchen minions make great sandwiches," she said, taking a bite of chicken salad.

"I'll remember to thank them."

At some point during the day, either Luis or Eduardo would fill the refrigerator and cupboards with food, much of it readymade. She wasn't entirely sure it didn't come from the palace itself. The King of Montoro had a wonderful cook staff. But she decided the mystery was exciting and she didn't want to know how it magically appeared. She liked that it just did.

"What do we do now?" she asked, taking another bite.

Juan Carlos's throat worked, as he tipped a water bottle back and took a sip. He wiped the back of his hand across his mouth and turned to her, his eyes dark and searching. "I don't know. I think we've exhausted all possibilities. Where else is there to look?"

She had to agree. They'd searched the entire grounds—the prairies, the hills, the outer buildings—and found nothing. "The art could be anywhere and we'd never know it. There are no clues and sadly those secrets have been buried along with your family members."

He nodded. "At least the artwork didn't fall into the hands of the dictator, which was their main intent. I can't say I'm not disappointed. I thought we'd find something, a clue, some hint that would lead us to it. I can only hope it is found one day."

"I'm sorry, Juan Carlos." She set her sandwich down and brought her lips to his mouth. It was a chaste kiss, one of commiseration.

Instantly, his arms wound around her shoulders and he tugged, pulling her practically on top of him, deepening the kiss. "You're the only woman who can make me feel better," he murmured.

A pulse throbbed in her neck. She loved hearing his sweet words, even though they might be some of the last she'd hear from him. Soon, when the search was finally concluded, she'd have to say goodbye to him and all that they'd meant to each other in this short span of time. Yet, right now, she wanted to make him feel better—but she couldn't do it here. Out in the open. "We should go," she said. "Luis is watching."

He kissed her again, and then lifted himself up, pulling his phone out of his pocket. He spent a few seconds texting someone and then returned to her. "He's not watching anymore."

"Juan Carlos! What did you say to him?"

His lips twitched. "I told him to retreat one hundred yards and turn his head away from the Jeep for twenty minutes."

"You didn't!" Her face instantly burned. Her pride was stung. "He's going to know."

Juan Carlos touched her face gently, his fingertips on her cheeks, calming her. "Sweetheart, any man who sees how I look at you *knows*. Luis won't say a word."

"But I'll know he knows."

"It's beautiful here, Portia. And I need you. Do you not need me, too?"

His words worked magic on her. Yes, she needed him, too. She nodded. "But—"

He kissed away her doubts and then lowered her onto the blanket. His mouth was brutally tender, claiming her with each stroke of the tongue as soul-wrenching groans escaped his throat.

Thrills ran up and down her body as he exposed her to the sun's rays. The scent of fresh water and clear skies combined made her forget her inhibitions. She'd never made love outdoors and she only wanted to experience it with this one exciting man.

Firelight created jumping shadows across the living room walls. Juan Carlos sat with Portia beside him on the sofa as they watched Duchess bathe a kitten, her tongue taking long swipes across its furry body. The kitten took a playful swing or two at mama cat, but Duchess didn't relent. She used one paw to hold her charge down, determined to finish the job and lick away the grime of the day before moving on to her next one. She cleansed and fed her young diligently. Duchess, for all her wildness, was a good mama cat.

"You're quiet tonight," Portia said. "Still thinking about the missing art treasure?"

That was part of it. His failure to find it bothered him. He'd been so certain that there were clues here on the property and yet, he felt as if he was missing something important. He couldn't say what, but deep down in his bones he still believed the answers were here.

Yet most of his thoughts concerned Portia. They'd exhausted their search and there was nothing to keep them on the farm any longer. Tomorrow they would head back to Del Sol and then Portia would return to the States. Eventually. Unless he could convince her to stay.

"I'm thinking about us," he answered honestly.

Portia put her head on his shoulder. "What about us?" she asked, her smooth-as-velvet voice tapping into his heart. At least she didn't say, *there is no us.* She recognized that they were edging toward a precarious cliff.

Three sharp raps at the door interrupted their conversation. He gave it a glance and waited for the next two knocks, which would signal him that all was well. Those two knocks came and Juan Carlos rose, striding to the door. "It's either Luis or Eduardo," he said over his shoulder to reassure Portia, and then opened the door. "Eduardo. I trust everything is all right?"

"Yes. But I have something of interest I thought you would want to hear right now."

Eduardo glanced at Portia, who was now sitting on the edge of the sofa, her eyes round with curiosity. "Regarding?"

"Your search, Your Majesty."

Juan Carlos swung the door open wider. "Come in."

"Your Highness," he said to Portia as he made his way inside the room.

"Eduardo." She granted him a beautiful smile, most likely grateful it wasn't his counterpart, Luis, seeking them out. He could see the relief in her eyes. This afternoon, making love under blue skies behind the Jeep, Portia had let go her inhibitions and made a memory that would live forever in his mind. But afterward his Portia had gone on and on about Luis, asking how she could ever face him again.

Juan Carlos had succeeded in kissing away her worries.

"Would you like to sit down?" Portia asked.

"No, thank you. I didn't mean to interrupt." Eduardo regarded the kittens, his expression softening.

"Duchess is coming around," Portia said, her eyes glittering.

One look at Eduardo and the cat's back arched, and a low mewling hiss sprang from her mouth.

Portia rolled her eyes. "*Slowly* she's coming along. She should know better than to bite the hand that feeds her. Sorry, Eduardo. And how are your hands?"

He waved them in the air. "They are fine, Princess. No need to worry."

"What did you find out of interest, Eduardo?" he asked. "Something about the search?"

"Yes, Your Highness. You gave me the list of names on the graves at the Montoro family cemetery."

"Yes, I committed many of them to memory." He'd tasked Eduardo with contacting his uncle Rafe and alerting him about the cemetery. Juan Carlos wanted those family plots cleaned up and the headstones that were damaged beyond repair to be replaced as soon as possible.

"Yes, well, I spoke with your uncle, as you asked. He has no knowledge of those family members or that there even was a Montoro cemetery on the grounds. Not one name seemed to jar his memory."

"We didn't have first names. We only found initials on the headstones. It doesn't matter if he remembered the names or not. We will have that cemetery restored."

"There's more."

Juan Carlos nodded. "I'm listening."

"Your uncle claims that as a rite of passage, every Montoro had the privilege of being buried in the family mausoleum in Alma, whether rich or poor. If they were related to Montoro and had bloodlines, it was an honor to be buried there."

"Yes, I know that. But surely during Tantaberra's reign, that wouldn't hold true anymore. After the war, everything changed. I assumed those graves were there because Tantaberra controlled even where a person would lay to rest."

Portia walked up to take his hand. "But Juan Carlos, think about some of the dates on the headstones. Many were pre-Tantaberra."

He gave it a moment of thought, his mind clicking back to the headstones. "You're right. There were at least four that I remember that dated back to the 1920s and '30s. Before the war, before Tantaberra."

"Yes," Portia said, her voice reaching a higher pitch. "And those initials might've been used to throw people off. They'd have no real way of investigating who was laid to rest there."

"Hold on a second," Juan Carlos said, pulling out his phone. He clicked over to the list he'd brought with him of the known art pieces missing from the palace. His heart racing, he located the titles.

"*Joven Amelia.* J.A. were the initials on one of the headstones," he said. "It means Young Amelia. *Almas Iguales.* A.I. was another set of initials. The sculpture is called *Equal Souls* in English. And then there is *Dos Rios.*"

"D.R. I remember that one," Portia said. "I thought he was a doctor."

"There's a painting called *Dos Rios* that's missing," he said. "Portia, you said it yourself this afternoon, the secrets have been buried along with my family members.

But I don't think there are any family members buried in the cemetery."

"You think the artwork is buried there." Portia's voice was breathless and eager.

"It's a long shot, Princess. I think the cemetery is bogus. It was the family's way of protecting the art from Tanta-berra. We have to find out. Eduardo, get in touch with Luis. We'll need a bulldozer, but for now, round up shovels and some high-powered lights. I'm going tonight."

"Oh, Juan Carlos, do you really think you've found it?"

"*We* found it, Portia. You're as much a part of this as I am."

Portia nodded, an excited smile teasing her lips. "I'll go change my clothes."

"Portia," he said, "are you sure you want to go? If I'm wrong, it will be pretty gruesome."

"If you really want to see *gruesome* try and stop me, Your Highness."

He grinned. "That's right. You're not a wimpy princess."

He was glad. It wouldn't feel right going on this search without her by his side.

Whatever they found.

Seven

"I really know how to show a lady a good time, don't I?" With shovel in hand, Juan Carlos dug at the foot of a grave alongside Eduardo and Luis as the high beams of two cars cast the cemetery in an unearthly glow.

Dirt flew through the air and landed at the toes of her boots. If she weren't so excited, she'd be totally creeped out. "I can't think of anywhere else I'd rather be," she countered honestly.

Even her embarrassment with Luis had been forgotten.

"I can help out," she said, "when anyone wants to take a break."

Eduardo covered his laughter with a grunt.

Juan Carlos slanted her a be-serious look. "I'll keep that in mind, Princess."

Luis was too busy digging to look up.

She wrapped her arms around her sides as the night air became chillier. She'd refused Juan Carlos's suggestion to sit it out in the car and so she stood watching, waiting.

They were digging up the grave of J. A. Molina. The headstone dated the death to 1938.

After ten minutes of silent digging, she heard a thump. Eduardo's shovel smacked against something solid. Thump, thump. "I hit something, Your Highness," Eduardo said.

"Let's keep digging," Juan Carlos said. There was a

boyish tone to his excitement. "It shouldn't be long now before we know."

The men worked twice as fast now, focusing their efforts. The scraping sounds of shovels against wood filled the quiet night.

"Portia, will you get the flashlight and shine it down here."

The men were five feet below ground level now and working furiously.

She grabbed the biggest flashlight she could find and stood as close as possible over the grave site, sending beams of light down. Portia's heart sank. "It's a coffin, isn't it?"

"Maybe," Juan Carlos said. Under her flashlight, his eager eyes had lost some of their gleam. A layer of dirt remained on top of the box, and he used his gloved hands to swipe it off, searching for any hint of what lay inside. He found nothing written. "Let's bring it up."

It took some doing, but the three men hoisted the box up and set it on a patch of flat ground.

"Hand me the ax," Juan Carlos ordered. He made the sign of the cross over his chest. "And may God forgive us."

Luis handed Juan Carlos the tool and he carefully began to hack at the very edges of the coffin. Each blow of the ax brought the mystery closer and closer to an end. Eduardo used his shovel to help pry the lid of the box open.

It was time. Their work was nearly over. Juan Carlos hesitated a moment, drew breath into his lungs and then glanced at her. "Ready?"

She nodded.

"You might want to look away," he said.

"No, I will be fine with whatever we find." Her eye twitched, closing in a wink.

Juan Carlos stared at her. Perhaps he was equally as nervous as she was. With his gloved hands, he lifted the hacked lid. She beamed the flashlight on the contents, her heart thumping hard.

"There's no corpse." His voice elevated, he continued, "But there's something in here."

She held her breath, her pulse jumping in her veins. He unfolded a sheath, and found another box, no more than two by three feet, this one carved and quite ornate. He lifted it out and she shined the flashlight on it. *Joven Amelia* was etched in golden lettering on top.

Juan Carlos's hand shook. "It's here. Thank God," he said. Setting the box down on the ground, he kneeled, and she took a place beside him. He took great care to remove his filthy gloves and then opened the latch and lifted the lid.

Inside, surrounded by lush black velvet, there was a painting of a little girl, no more than ten years old, playing near the seashore with a much younger sister. The canvas was secured, not rolled up as one might expect, but mounted to a frame as if taken from the palace in a hurry. Portia would have to inspect it thoroughly and do some research, but she was almost certain that it was genuine, given the great pains the royal family had taken to hide the painting decades ago.

"It's beautiful," she said. "She is Young Amelia."

Tears welled in Juan Carlos's eyes. "We did it, Portia. We found the missing treasures."

"Yes," she breathed, her heart swelling. "Yes."

"Eduardo, Luis, come see."

Taking her hand, Juan Carlos rose and tugged her up with him. Once standing, he wrapped his arms around her waist and drew her close, so they were hip to hip. Joy beamed in her heart. It was a monumental occasion and she found no reason for pretense. As Juan Carlos had said, the way he looked at her left little room for doubt of his feelings, anyway. They were lovers. It was hard to disguise.

The bodyguards peered at the painting in its casing. Both seemed awed and a little surprised to be looking at a royal masterpiece lost for generations.

"Congratulations, Your Majesty," Eduardo said.

"Alma's precious treasures have been restored," Luis said.

The two men shook the king's hand. There was pride and resolve in all of their eyes.

Eduardo turned to her. "Princess Portia, congratulations to you, as well. It is a great find."

"Thank you, Eduardo. That's very kind of you to say." She stepped forward and placed a kiss on his cheek. "I'm thrilled to have helped in a small way."

Eduardo blushed, but gave no indication he was alarmed by her affectionate display. A smile tugged at his lips, bringing her a rush of friendly warmth inside.

Juan Carlos got right down to business again. "I would like you to secure the grounds tonight. When the bulldozers arrive, we will resume digging in the morning. Assemble a team. I would like to have all the art secured by the end of the day tomorrow, if possible."

"Yes, Your Highness," Luis said. "It will be done."

The men turned to do their tasks, and Juan Carlos took her hand and began dragging her away from the stream of lights. "Come with me, sweetheart," he said.

"Where are we going?"

"To bed, as soon as I can arrange it," he said. "But for now, this will have to do."

He pulled her behind the cars, out into the darkness under the stars. And the next thing she knew, Juan Carlos's hands were about her and she was flying, sailing through the air, spinning around and around. "We did it, Princess. We did it."

"Yes, yes, we did." Laughter spilled from her lips and a lightness of spirit filled her.

"This is an amazing moment. I'm glad to be sharing it with you," he said.

Her smile broadened. "I feel the same way, Juan Carlos. I'm bursting inside."

He brought her down to earth gently, her boots gracing the sacred grounds. And his lips sought hers instantly, kissing her mouth, chin, cheeks and forehead. His hands sifted through her hair and his dark, luscious eyes bored into her. "Do you have any idea how much I love you, Portia? I do. I love you, Princess. With all my heart."

"Oh, Juan Carlos, I love you, too." And there it was. Her truth. Her honest feelings poured out of her in this instant of happiness and joy. She could no longer hide away from the sensations rocking her from head to toe. The words she spoke were not damning, but blissful and joyous. She loved Juan Carlos Salazar II, King Montoro of Alma.

"You do? You love me?" His grin spoke to her heart in a language all its own. His was the sweetest of tones, as if he was in total awe of her love.

She nodded eagerly. "I love you."

He lifted her up and twirled her around once more before he set her down. His kiss this time made her dizzier than a dozen spins in his arms. His mouth claimed her, his lips demanding, his tongue penetrating through to sweep in and conquer. Her knees wobbled and she sought his sturdy shoulders for balance, her monumental declaration swaying both of them.

"Oh, Portia, my love. I cannot think of a life without you. Marry me. Be my wife. Be with me forever."

The words rang in her ears. It wasn't as if she hadn't expected them to come, but the surprise came only in her answer. "Yes, Juan Carlos. I will marry you."

The next morning, Portia woke in Juan Carlos's arms, opening her eyes to a face she had come to love. Handsome, breathtaking and dynamic. He was a man who got things done. He'd certainly pursued her to the point of her complete compliance. How could she not fall in love with this man?

"Good morning, fiancée," he said, kissing the tip of her nose.

"Hello, my love," she said.

They'd celebrated in this very bed well into the night. There was champagne and candles and bone-melting caresses.

As she plopped her head against the pillow, the sheets pulled away, exposing her bare shoulders. Her eyes lifted to the ceiling, focusing on tiles that were chipping away. The farmhouse, old and neglected as it was, had undeniable charm. She sighed. "Is this real?"

"So real," Juan Carlos said. "Here, feel my heart."

He grasped her hand and placed it on his chest. Under her fingertips, life-sustaining beats pulsed through his veins. "I am real. A man who loves a woman."

"But you are the king of Alma."

"And you are the princess of Samforstand...we are meant to be, sweetheart. Can you not see how perfect this is? Fate has stepped in and brought the two of us together. I can only marry a woman of royal blood. And that's you." He brought her hand to his lips and tenderly kissed one finger, then another and another. "When I became king, marrying was the last thing on my mind. But then I saw you at the coronation and all bets were off."

"And what if I weren't a princess? Then what would you have done?"

"I would have..." He hesitated and sighed, bringing her up and over his body so that she straddled his thighs. He nipped at her lips and wove his fingers through her hair, eyeing the locks as if they were made of gold. "Luckily, I don't have that burden."

"No, you don't," she said, taking his hand and placing it on her chest. The heat of his palm warmed her breast and she squeezed her hand over his. "Feel my heart."

His eyes filled with hunger and every cell in her body reacted to his sensual touch. "You are wicked, Princess."

She chuckled. "You bring it out in me."

"You see, we *are* a perfect match."

"Are we?" She nibbled on her lip. She'd disobeyed her hard and fast rule of not falling for a high-profile man. You couldn't get much higher than king. Was she destined to fame through association even though it's the last thing she wanted?

"Let me show you again, so that you will never doubt it."

His hands on her hips, he gently guided her over him and they welcomed the dawn with their bodies and hearts joined as one.

But her doubts remained, locked and hidden away, even as she agreed to marry him. Even as she claimed her love for him. Half an hour later, she was showered and dressed. She and Juan Carlos ate a quick breakfast of cereal and fruit, both anxious to get back to the cemetery site this morning. But Portia couldn't forget her six charges. She walked into the living area with bowls of water and cat food in her hands and set them down by the fireplace hearth, where Duchess had taken up residence. "Here you go, girl."

Duchess no longer looked at her with frightened eyes. She had at one time been domesticated, and she was beginning to remember her life before hunger and fear had changed her. Portia kneeled and watched the cat rise, stretch her neck and shake out her limbs, and then walk over to the water. She lapped furiously as five balls of fluff scrambled to be near her, one kitten losing his balance and plopping half his body into the bowl. He jumped back, as if hit by a jolt, and gave himself a few shakes. Tiny drops of water sprinkled Portia's clothes.

She giggled and pressed her hand to the top of the little one's head. Silky fur tickled her palm. "You are a feisty one."

Juan Carlos strode into the room. "Are you ready to go, sweetheart?"

She stood. "Yes. I can't wait to see what else we uncover."

According to Eduardo, two bulldozers and a full crew were working furiously this morning. In the middle of the night, he'd called upon and assembled a team of men he could trust with this secret. Soon, the entire country would know about the hidden artwork. What a story to tell.

Last night, Juan Carlos had shared his hopes of putting many of these treasures on display for Alma citizens as well as tourists who would come to view the find. It would be nothing short of a boon for the country. The restoration of the artwork would instill pride and honor in a country once diminished and downtrodden by a dictator. First, though, Portia, along with a Latin art specialist, would have to verify that the pieces were not fakes.

By the time they reached the site, half the graveyard was dug up. Dust swirled through the air from the many mounds of dirt dotting the cemetery. Ten men with shovels and axes were hoisting boxes up from the graves. Luis, with pen and pad in hand, was making an inventory list. As ordered, none of the boxes had been opened.

Juan Carlos helped her down from the Jeep. He took her hand and they walked to where Luis stood next to a gravestone marked with the initials P.P. Tasked with documenting and photographing each headstone before the box was brought up, Luis lifted his head to greet them.

"Your Highness, Princess," he said. "We have twelve boxes already accounted for. As you can see, we have more to do. We've placed them inside the tent over there," he said, pointing to a room-size tent set up outside the cemetery under guard by two men, "and they are ready for you to open."

"Thank you, Luis," Juan Carlos said. "Your men are working faster than I thought. Now, if you'll come with me, I'll need you to document what we find as I open the boxes."

"I'll take the photos," Portia said.

Luis handed over his digital camera and nodded. "Thank you, Your Highness."

Excitement stirred in her belly. To be a part of this find was a dream come true. How many dreams was one person allowed in a lifetime? All this joy in such a short span of time? She'd found adventure and love where she'd least expected it, in the arms of a king.

Inside the tent, Juan Carlos opened box after box, carefully removing the pieces for documentation. Oil paintings, sculptures, bronzed statues and the famed ancient Alma tiara had been locked away and hidden from the world for decades. Portia photographed everything, carefully making mental notes of the pieces she would research for authentication.

They worked alongside the men, until all the pieces were uncovered and the mock cemetery was emptied out. By late afternoon, they'd unearthed twenty-two boxes in all, the grave sites now nothing but pockmarks in the earth.

Juan Carlos climbed to the top of a pile of dirt in the center of the graveyard, his boots spread out, his voice booming to the loyal men who had labored here. As he spoke, shovels were held still, conversations died down. "The Montoro family cemetery has done its job to preserve what is sovereign to our country. You are all a part of Alma history now and I thank you for your hard work today. Until these items are authenticated, I would ask for your silence. Luis and Eduardo have assured me all of you can be trusted. The next step is to transport these pieces back to the palace in the trucks you arrived in. Again, thank you all for your diligence."

Juan Carlos jumped down from the dirt hill and once again, Portia was reminded of how well he fit the position of king. He was a true diplomat and leader. A man to be admired. Staunch in his beliefs and fair-minded…she was sure if the clocks were turned back in time to when Alma was last ruled by a king, he would have reigned over his people justly.

"What are you staring at?" he asked, approaching her.

She shook off her thoughts and smiled. "How handsome you are with dirt on your face."

He grinned. "I could say the same about you, Princess. The smudges on your face only make you more beautiful." He touched her nose, right cheek and forehead.

Goodness, she'd never considered what the hours of dust and grime had done to her fair complexion. "I must be a mess."

"Nothing a hot bubble bath wouldn't cure, and I'm volunteering to scrub your back," he whispered.

"I'll take you up on that, Your Highness."

And shortly after, they left the graveyard and returned to the farmhouse.

They had one night left to share here. And Portia was sure, Juan Carlos would make it memorable, bubble bath and all.

Portia was too much in love to think about her future and how marrying Juan Carlos would affect her life and her career. She had no details to cling to, only love, and it would have to see her through the tough decisions she would have to make. Now, as she sat at a long dressed table in the palace's elegant dining room, she gazed first at her secret fiancé seated at the helm. Dressed in a charcoal-black suit, he was beaming and full of determination. He appeared ready to make the announcement to his family. Rafe and Emily sat across from her with her friend Maria and Alex Ramon.

Gabriel and his wife, Serafia, sat to her left, along with Bella and James. James's little girl, Maisey, was holding tight to her chest a princess doll dressed in aqua-blue with hair the color of glistening snow.

"It's a lovely doll, Maisey," Portia commented, smiling at the child.

"She looks a lot like you, Portia," Bella commented. "I'm just noticing the likeness."

Maisey's curious eyes shifted to Portia and the girl giggled. It was true that she shared a resemblance with a famous cartoon character that all young girls seemed to love.

Juan Carlos covered Portia's hand, entwining their fingers. "Ah, but Portia is a one-of-a-kind princess."

All those close to Juan Carlos were here. He'd invited them for dinner tonight under the pretense of disclosing the facts around the graveyard find. Only he and Portia knew the truth.

"Before the meal is served, a toast is in order," he said. "We have much to celebrate tonight."

Waiters poured champagne into crystal flutes.

Once all the bubbles settled, Juan Carlos rose. "Thank you, cousins and friends, for joining me tonight. We all have much to be thankful for. As you know, with Portia's help, we have found the missing pieces of art at the Montoro family farm. Yes, it's true, we dug up mock graves to unearth the treasures. The finds are yet to be authenticated, but we are fairly certain our ancestors wouldn't have gone to such extreme measures to hide fake artwork. Portia will do the preliminary research on the items we've found and under her advisement we will also hire an expert to verify each piece.

"But that is not why I've called you here today. I have

something more personal to share with you." He turned to Portia, offering his hand. She took it and rose, warmth traveling up her cheeks. All eyes were on her and the king.

Juan Carlos went down on one knee, and gasps erupted from the diners at the table. She had no idea he would go traditional on her in front of his family. But how silly of her not to think it. Juan Carlos was a man of tradition and so as she gazed into his gleaming dark eyes, she began to tremble.

"Princess Portia, you know I love you with all of my heart. I have since the moment I laid eyes on you."

Tears wet her eyes.

"I have one precious thing left of my childhood and now, I am offering it to you." He reached into his jacket pocket and came up with a diamond ring, the stone so brilliant, it caught the chandelier light and virtually illuminated the room. "This was my mother's wedding ring," he said, his voice tight. "And here before our family and close friends, I ask you to wear it and become my wife. Portia, Princess of Samforstand, will you marry me?"

Not even a breath could be heard in the roomful of people.

Her cheeks were moist with tears as she nodded. "Yes, yes. Of course I'll marry you, Juan Carlos. I am honored to wear your mother's ring."

Her hand shook as he slid the ring that once belonged to his mother onto her finger. He stared at the ring, his eyes deeply reverent, and then grinned wide, looking foolishly happy. With the pads of his thumbs, he wiped at her tears and then took her in a kiss that nearly muffled the screams of delight and applause coming from behind her.

After the kiss, they were both swarmed with handshakes and hugs.

She was beside herself with happiness. The love and acceptance she experienced from his family and friends was more than she'd ever expected. There were no, *Are you sures?* or *This has happened so fasts*, but rather, "Congratulations" and "You two are perfect for each other."

After everyone returned to their seats, Juan Carlos lifted his glass of champagne. "Please join me in welcoming my fiancée, Portia, to our family. Today, she has made me the happiest man on earth."

Glasses clinked and sips were taken.

Portia's heart swelled. All doubts about her future were laid to rest. She and Juan Carlos would work things out. They would find a way to keep each other happy and not lose their own identity. She would be his wife in all ways. She would one day bear his child, an heir to the throne of Alma.

She locked the thought deep inside her heart and it filled her with joy.

"Jasmine, yes. It's true, it's true. I'm engaged to Juan Carlos. I wanted to tell you before news of our engagement reached the States. The king's assistant will be speaking to the media tomorrow to share our engagement news." Portia held the cell phone to her ear as she looked out the window of Juan Carlos's master suite in the palace. The king's room had a view of the gardens below, with its expertly groomed fall flowers.

"Congratulations, Portia. Wow. It's hard to believe. The king moves fast, doesn't he?" Jasmine asked, a little bit in awe.

"Yes, he does," she said softly, focusing on a row of red carnations growing in the garden. They were hardy this time of year. "He's quite persuasive when he wants something. That's why he'll be a great king and not just a figurehead. After news of our find comes out, the country will see how much Alma means to him. They'll rally behind him, and he'll be… Jas, forgive me, I'm rambling, aren't I?"

"Oh, my gosh, Portia. I hear it in your voice. You're really in love, aren't you?"

"He's amazing, Jas. And I resisted him as long as I could, but Juan Carlos…well, when you meet him, you'll see what I mean."

"I'm going to meet him?" She pictured her friend's eyes snapping to attention.

"Of course, silly. At the wedding. Jasmine, I want you by my side. I know it's a lot to ask, since the wedding will be held in Alma, but I'd be thrilled if you'd be my maid of honor."

"Portia…this is… Of course I'll be your maid of honor! I wish you could see me jumping up and down right now."

She chuckled. "I've got the image in my head. Just be careful. The last time you jumped for joy, you crashed into my dining table and nearly broke your leg."

"Okay, I've stopped jumping now," she said, out of breath. "This is all so very exciting."

"I can hardly believe it myself. Juan Carlos wants to be married, like, yesterday, so I think it's going to happen as soon as we can put all the pieces together."

"Count on me to help."

"Thank you. I was hoping you'd say that and I'm glad you're going to be in my wedding. Right now, I'm working on an art authentication project that will take me until the end of the week to finish. I should be home in three days. Then it'll be full steam ahead with wedding plans."

"I can't wait to see you. I have a million questions for you."

"And I don't have a million answers. But it'll work out," Portia said, taking a deep breath. "It has to. Have to run now. Love you, Jas."

"Love you, too," her assistant said, and then hung up.

"What don't you have a million answers to?" Juan Carlos was suddenly beside Portia at the window. His arms around her waist, he took the cell phone from her hand and turned her to face him. She looked into curious, warm dark eyes.

"All of this?" she said. She couldn't lie. The roller coaster was going fast and she was holding on for dear life. "I don't know how this will all work out. I have a career, a life and a job on both US coasts. As it is, I'm not home much."

He lifted her chin and tilted his head. She braced herself for the onslaught of his kiss. When he held her this way and gazed at her, she turned into a puddle of mush. The kiss was long and leisurely. He took his time with her and every bone in her body melted. Yes, her fiancé knew how to devastate.

"As long as we love each other," he said, "the obstacles won't be too great. I don't expect you to give up your work, Princess. I won't demand anything of you but your love."

When he spoke so sincerely, she believed him. She saw her future bright and clear. Nothing was more powerful than their shared love. "You have that, Your Highness."

His fingertips traced the outline of her lips. "I heard you say you'll be going in three days."

"Yes," she said. "When I'm through researching and authenticating what I can of the Montoro art collection, I'll head back to the States. I have appointments to keep."

"And you'll look into wedding protocols from your native Samforstand?"

"Yes, I know that's important to you. It is to me, too."

"Our union should reflect both of our heritages and royal traditions. The wedding must be a melding of both of our countries. The sooner, the better, my love. I can hardly stand the thought of you leaving." He sent her head swirling with another earth-shattering kiss.

"Well," she said, licking her lips. "We do have three

more days together. And nights." She arched her brows and slanted her head, playing coy.

Juan Carlos took the bait. With a growl, he lifted her up and carried her to the bed, unceremoniously dropping her so that she bounced on the mattress. A chuckle ripped from her lips. "Your Highness," she said, staring at the bulge growing in his pants. "It's half past eleven in the morning."

"Princess, I don't see a problem with that, do you?"

She shook her head, giggling. It didn't take much to tempt her new fiancé and she loved that about him.

He climbed onto the bed and Portia spent the next hour making up for the time she and Juan Carlos would be apart.

Eight

"Wow, Portia, you look beautiful in this dress. I think it's the one," Jasmine said, nodding her head in approval. Her friend was having a grand time getting her in and out of wedding dresses, much to the dismay of the shop owner who stood just outside the dressing room, hoping to be called in to aid and assist in the fitting.

Portia stood on a pedestal platform gazing at her reflection in the three-way mirror in the tiny wedding shop in Santa Monica. "You said that about the last three gowns I've tried on."

"I can't help it. They all look amazing on you. But this one with the ivory tulle and Swarovski crystals." Jasmine sighed. "It's heavenly."

"It is lovely," Portia said, admiring the lines of the dress. "It's such a big decision."

"I'll say. It's not every day a friend of mine marries a king. Princess or not."

Portia chuckled.

Once word of the new king of Alma's American fiancée had hit the Los Angeles newsstands, Portia had been inundated with offers of gown fittings, hair and makeup, photographers and wedding planners. She'd had requests for radio and television talk shows. She'd refused them all, trying to scale down the hoopla. She hadn't expected to be crowded at the airport by the paparazzi, or followed home for that matter. Once again, her personal life was under the spotlight.

None of it mattered, though. She was so deeply in love with Juan Carlos, the unwanted attention was manageable. On some level, she understood the public's desire for a fairy-tale love story. Ghastly news reports of wars, poverty and chilling murders needed some balance. The country craved something positive and lovely to grasp onto, and a newly crowned king marrying a princess, both of whom had lived in America, fit the bill.

Portia stepped out of the gown and redressed in her own clothes before letting Amelia of Amelia's Elegance into the dressing room. "Thank you for your time," Portia said to the shop owner. "I will keep this gown in mind. It's certainly beautiful."

Jasmine was careful handing the wedding dress over to Amelia. "This is my favorite, with the chapel length veil."

"I agree. It's certainly fitting for a princess," the shop owner said, nodding her head. "It's from a most talented designer. I shall put it on hold for you, if you'd like?"

Jasmine nodded. "Yes, the princess would like that."

Portia did a mental eye roll. Jasmine loved using the princess card for special favors.

"Your Highness, thank you for considering my shop for your wedding needs."

"You're welcome. I appreciate your time. You do have some stunning things here."

Amelia beamed with pride. "Thank you. We try to accommodate our clients with only the highest quality material and design."

"We have a few other stops to make, but I will personally call you when the princess makes up her mind," Jasmine said.

Amelia thanked them and walked them out the door.

"Did you love the dress?" Jasmine asked. "A bride has

to fall in love with her dress. They say as soon as she puts the right one on, she knows. Did you know?"

"Well, I did like it."

"But you didn't love it?"

Portia got into the front seat of Jasmine's car. "No, I didn't *love* it."

Luckily, no one had followed her to the dress shop. Jasmine got into the driver's seat and glanced around. "Did you hear? Rick Manning just got engaged to the daughter of a United States senator. It's all over the news. They claim to be crazy about each other."

Rick Manning, an A-list movie star, was dubbed the man least likely to ever marry. Handsome and charming and very much a ladies' man. "Yes, it was all over the news this morning. I've met Eliza Bennington. She's a nice person."

"Well, you can thank them both. Luckily, the tabloids have dropped you like a hot potato. At least, until more royal wedding news is announced. The dogs are on a different scent right now."

"I don't envy them. It's no fun having your every move analyzed."

"I hear you," Jasmine said, and pulled out of the parking spot. "Are you hungry?"

"Starving. Let's have lunch."

"Okay, but afterward, the great wedding dress search goes on."

Portia agreed to that plan and looked out the window. Jasmine was taking her maid of honor duties seriously. The truth was, Portia had a hundred loose ends to tie up before the wedding, and she missed Juan Carlos like crazy. They spoke at least twice a day since she'd left him at the airport in Alma.

"You are perfect for me, Princess. Always remember

that," were his last words to her as she boarded his private airplane.

It was after six in the evening when Jasmine dropped her off at home. She climbed the few steps of her one-level Brentwood condo, knowing she had another hunt on her hands. She'd promised Juan Carlos she'd look up royal wedding protocols from Samforstand. She'd been too busy with rescheduling her work appointments and dress shopping to dig into her old files until now.

She dropped her purse on the couch and then strode to the fridge and grabbed a Coke. Sipping from the can, she walked into her bedroom and pulled out the old cedar trunk from the back of her walk-in closet. The trunk held the few remaining things she had left of her parents.

Unlatching the lid, she found a massive amount of papers, deeds, bank account records and folders upon folders of news clippings about her parents when they were a young royal couple in exile. She lifted out an article written about them from the *New York Times*, just days before the tragic car accident that claimed their lives. Her eyes misted as she looked at a picture of the loving couple that accompanied the article. Her father was decked out in royal regalia with her mother by his side. They were young and happy and it hurt her heart still to look at them and think about all they had lost.

Her mother's wedding ring was in its original sapphire-blue velvet box, her father's tie clips and a gold wedding band were stored in a polished walnut case. She assumed most of their other possessions were sold to keep her comfortable and pay for her expenses. She'd been raised by her grandmother Joanna. But now all she had was her great-aunt, Margreta, who was a little senile. Portia paid for her care in a nursing home and visited her whenever she could.

As the evening wore on, she pored over every piece of paper in the trunk. She read every article and viewed every picture taken. Yet nowhere could she find any research that dated back to her great-grandparents' era of rule before they'd migrated to the United States after World War II. Surely, there had to be something? Having lost her parents early in life, she had only a fragmentary account of her heritage from her grandmother. Grandma Joanna hadn't liked to talk about the old days. It was too painful, a past wrought with the loss of her only son. Portia's questions about her parents were met with hushed tones and sadness and she'd never really learned much about them. She did remember her mother's bright smile and her father's light blue eyes. But even now, she wondered if those were true memories, or just recollections of the pictures she'd seen.

Her cell phone rang and a name popped up on the screen. She answered before the second ring. "Juan Carlos." She sighed.

His baritone voice drifted to her over thousands of miles. "Hello, Princess. I had to hear your voice once more before I started my day. I hope I didn't wake you."

She glanced at the clock. It was 8:00 a.m. in Alma. "No, not at all. I'm doing some research right now. I'm glad you called. How are you?"

"Besides missing you, I'm doing well. I'm scheduled to do a television interview later this morning. All of Alma is rejoicing over our art find, sweetheart. But I have a feeling the interviewer is more interested in our engagement. I'm sure I will be barraged with questions about our wedding."

"I'm sure you can handle it, Your Highness."

"What I can't handle is not being with my perfect princess. When will you be returning to me?"

"Give me a week, Juan Carlos," she said. "I need the time to get some things in order."

"Sounds like an eternity."

"For me, too, but I have a lot to accomplish. Jasmine

has been persistent. We are very close to choosing a wedding gown."

"I can't wait to see you in it. No matter which you choose you'll be beautiful. But what have you decided about your work?"

"I've managed to take a three months' leave of absence. I'm thinking of relocating to Europe. There are many American art collectors living abroad who might need my services. I…I don't have it all figured out yet."

"Take your time, sweetheart. I want you to be happy with whatever you choose."

"Okay. Thank you."

"I've been thinking. How does a Christmas wedding sound?"

"A Christmas wedding?" She pictured lush holly wreaths, bright red poinsettias and twinkling lights decorating the palace. "Sounds heavenly. But it's less than two months away."

Her fiancé was eager to make her his wife. She couldn't complain, yet her mind spun. She had so very much to do.

"We can make it work, Portia."

"Yes, yes. Okay," she said, smiling. The idea was too tempting to pass up. "Let's have a Christmas wedding."

There was a pause, and she pictured him smiling. "I love you, Portia."

"I love you, too, Juan Carlos."

The nursing home smelled of lye soap and disinfectant. Yet somehow the word *sterile* didn't come to mind as Portia walked the halls toward her great-aunt Margreta's room. Her aunt had once told her, "The odors of old age are too strong to conceal." Sharp old bird, Aunt Margreta was, back in the day. But Portia never knew what she'd find when she visited. Some days, her great-aunt was lucid, her wits about her. And some days, it was as if she'd fallen into a dark hole and didn't know how to get out.

This kind of aging was a slow, eternally sad process. Yet, as Portia popped her head into her aunt's room, she was greeted with cheery buttercup-colored walls and fresh flowers. Aunt Margreta sat in a chair, reading a crime thriller. A good sign.

"Hello, Auntie," Portia said. "It's me, Portia."

Her aunt looked over her thick eyeglasses and hesitated a moment. "Portia?"

Her voice was weak, her body frail and thin. "Yes, it's me."

The old woman smiled. "Come in, dear." She put the book down on her lap. "Nice of you to visit."

Thank heaven. Her aunt was having a good day. Maybe now, she could gather information about the Lindstrom monarchy that Portia hadn't been able to find anywhere else. She'd used up every one of her massive tools of research, including going through newspaper archives searching for an inkling about her family's rule and traditions carried out in Samforstand. She found nothing, which was very odd, and that lack of information brought her here today. Maybe Aunt Margreta could shed some light. She was her grandmother's sister and had lived in the homeland before the war.

Portia pulled up a chair and sat down beside her. "How are you, Auntie?"

"I can't complain. Well, I could, but it would do no good. I'm old, Portia. And you," she said, gazing over her glasses again. "You are as beautiful as I remember."

Portia took her hand and smiled. Aunt Margreta's hands were always soft, the skin loose and smooth over the aging bones. At ninety-three years old, she was as physically fit as one could expect, but for daily bouts of arthritis. But her mind wasn't holding up as well as her body and that worried Portia. "So are you, Aunt Margreta. You're a beautiful lady."

She'd always been a sweet woman, though as Portia remembered, she'd also been feisty in her day and not always in agreement with her sister, Joanna. The two would argue when they thought Portia couldn't hear. She never knew what they argued about, but as soon as Portia would step into the room, they'd shoot each other a glare and stop arguing, pretending things were all fine and dandy. Which they were, most of the time. Portia missed her parents, but she'd never discount the love Grandma Joanna and Great-Aunt Margreta bestowed upon her. It was the least she could do for her aunt to see to her care here at Somerset Village.

"Auntie, are they treating you well here?"

She nodded. "I'm fine, dear. The food's better now. We have a new chef and he doesn't cut corners. You'll see. You'll stay for lunch?"

"Of course I will. I'm looking forward to it."

"Then I'll get dressed up and we'll go to the dining room later."

"Okay. Auntie, I have good news." She lifted her left hand and wiggled her fingers. "I'm engaged."

Margreta squeezed her eyes closed. "Is it to Johnny Valente? That boy wouldn't leave you alone when you were younger. I never liked him. "

Johnny Valente? Portia used to play with him in grade school, two decades ago. He was a bully who'd called her Polar Bear Portia, because of her light hair and skin tone. "Gosh no, Auntie. I never liked him, either." She hoped her aunt wasn't digressing. "I'm engaged to…" How should she say this? "I met this wonderful man when I was visiting Alma."

"What's Alma?"

"It's this beautiful island country just off the coast of

Spain. I met him at his coronation. Auntie, he was just crowned king. His name is Juan Carlos Salazar, King Montoro of Alma."

Aunt Margreta put her head down. "I see."

Her aunt's odd reaction surprised her. "Do you like my ring?"

She gave Portia's left hand a glance. "It sparkles."

"Yes, it does."

"But it looks old."

"Yes, I suppose it's at least fifty years old. It was his mother's ring. He...lost his family at a young age also."

"In a car accident, just like your mother and father?"

"Yes, the same way. We have a lot in common."

Pain entered her aunt's eyes. "That's terribly sad, isn't it?" Her aunt made a move to get up from the chair. "Is it time for lunch yet, dear?"

Portia's eye twitched. "Not yet, Auntie."

Her aunt relaxed back into her seat.

"Auntie, I have a question to ask you. It's very important to me, so please try to concentrate. I will be marrying a king and, well, since I also have royal bloodlines, my fiancé wants very much for me to carry out the protocols of my homeland during our wedding. Do you know where I might find that information? I can't seem to find anything about our family's rule before World War II."

Aunt Margreta put her head down again.

"Auntie, please. Try to remember."

"There are no protocols from the family," she said stoically.

"But surely...there have to be. Have you forgotten?"

"No, my dear. I have not forgotten. Your grandmother and I never saw eye to eye about this."

"About what, Auntie?"

Margreta stilled. "Tell no one. Tell no one. Tell no one," she repeated.

"Not even me, Auntie? What is it you're not supposed to tell?"

Margreta looked straight ahead, as if Portia wasn't there. As if she was going back in time, remembering. "Don't tell Portia. She must never know the truth."

"What?" Portia absorbed her words, but they didn't make any sense. "What do you mean, I must never know the truth? What truth?" Portia grabbed her aunt's hand, gently squeezing. "Auntie, please. You have to tell me."

Her aunt turned to stare at her. "You are not a princess," she said. Her voice was sorrowful, etched in pain and Portia's heart sunk at her earnest tone. "Our family never ruled in Samforstand. Your mother wasn't royalty and neither was my sister, Joanna. It's all a lie."

Surely, the old woman was having a senile episode. "But, Auntie, of course Grandmother was queen. She raised me. I would know if she wasn't."

Silence.

"Aunt Margreta, please?"

"Yes, you're right, dear. You would know. Never mind."

Her aunt's quick compliance confused her even more. And she started thinking back about her life and how she'd never really seen any official documents regarding the Lindstrom monarchy. They'd been figureheads, holding no great power, yet she'd never known much about her homeland. It wasn't talked about. It seemed from her recent research the monarchy started to take shape in the United States, just after World War II.

"Oh, my God," she murmured. Her body began to tremble as tears stung her eyes. "You're telling the truth, aren't you? I'm not a princess."

Her aunt's eyes softened, dimmed by sorrow. "I'm sorry, Portia dear."

"But how can I believe that? How can that possibly be true?"

Could she take the word of an elderly senile woman who went in and out of coherency?

"There's a diary," her aunt said. "Joanna kept a secret diary."

"Where?" Now Portia would get to the truth. "Where's the diary?"

Aunt Margreta pointed to the bookshelf against the far wall overflowing with books. "Behind Agatha Christie."

Portia strode over to the bookshelf. Her hands were shaking as she parted half a dozen mystery novels. She lifted a weathered, navy blue soft-covered book from the shelf and brought it close to her chest. It had no title on the cover. Her heart racing, she took her seat next to Aunt Margreta and began reading the words that made a lie out of her entire life.

Portia lay quietly on her sofa, a cool towel on her forehead. She'd cried a river full of tears and every cell in her body was now drained. Princess Portia Lindstrom of Samforstand no longer existed. She never had. She was a fraud, a fake. An imposter. How could her family do this to her? How could they have perpetrated a lie that would affect her entire life?

How cruel.

How unjust.

Damn the circumstances behind their decisions right now. Their bold blatant betrayal was all that mattered to her. How dare they mislead her and let her believe in the fairy tale? She wasn't the snow queen. Hell, once the truth got out, she'd be deemed the black witch.

She'd been involved in one scandal already and it had taken years to live that down. But this? This was too much. The press would devour her. They'd make her out to be the villain, a lying deceiving bitch out to ensnare a wealthy king.

The humiliation alone would destroy all the positive good Juan Carlos had done for his country.

She muffled another sob. She didn't have it in her to shed more tears.

Feeling empty, she closed her swollen eyes, unable to rid herself of the thoughts plaguing her. The lies she'd been told, the deceptions perpetrated by her family. What of her career? Most importantly, what would she do about Juan Carlos? He was king, and as king he was pledged to only marry a woman of royal heritage. It was his destiny. It was what the citizens of Alma expected. Juan Carlos was the most dutiful man she'd ever known. This would destroy their relationship.

The towel was removed from her head. "Feeling better yet? Want to get up?" Jasmine asked.

"Nooooo. I don't want to ever get up."

Jas sat down on the floor beside the sofa. "Hey, that doesn't sound like the Portia I know. You've been wallowing for two hours."

"I'm not the Portia you know. I'm not... I don't know who I am. And I have a right to wallow."

"Yes, it sucks. But Portia, you are you, no matter if you have the title of princess or not."

"It's just...it's just so darn humiliating. I feel like a fool. I feel, well, I feel like everything's a lie. My childhood, my upbringing, my friends."

"Hey, watch it there."

"You know I don't mean you."

Jasmine reached for her hand and squeezed. "I know."

"All the doors that have opened for me because of my title, Jas... Those people will think the worst of me. They'll think I deliberately deceived them to get ahead in my career."

"When in truth, we know, they were using you. They

wanted to be associated with a princess. So it was a trade-off. You have nothing to be ashamed of."

"I'm ashamed of everything."

"And angry."

"Yes, of course. I'm spitting mad at my family."

"I'm not justifying what they've done, honey. But they came to the States after the war destitute, and like so many immigrant families, they didn't know how they'd survive here. And, well, pretending to be royalty from a tiny country…"

"It's far-fetched. Yet they got away with it."

"Yes, your grandmother speaks of it in the diary. How scared they were and how confused things were in Europe and Scandinavia after the war. There was a lot of rebuilding and restructuring and things just fell into place for them. Surprisingly, they weren't questioned. After all, we didn't have close ties to the monarchy of Samforstand the way we did England. Your grandmother speaks of Americans having much to deal with after the war. Hundreds of thousands of soldiers were coming home. Work and housing in our country was scarce. Things were chaotic."

"But others found a way to survive without deception. They worked hard and built honest, decent lives for themselves." Portia hinged her body up from her prone position and swiveled to plant her feet on the floor. Sitting upright, her head spun a little. "I don't know what I'd do without you, Jasmine. Honestly, you're the only person I can trust with this."

Jasmine rose from the floor and the sofa cushions dipped as she came to sit next to her. Her friend hung her arm around Portia's shoulder and they sat there like that for long minutes, quiet.

"I'm scared, Jas."

"I know."

"I don't know who I am. I can't expect you to understand fully how I'm feeling, but suddenly, I'm confused about everything. My heart is aching so badly right now."

"That's why I'm here, Portia. You're not alone."

She rested her head on Jasmine's shoulder. "Thank you."

The house telephone rang. "Want me to get it?"

"No," she said to Jasmine. "I can't talk to anyone right now."

Jas nodded.

Shortly after that, her cell phone began ringing and she knew both calls were from Juan Carlos.

They spoke every evening before she went to bed. Never fail.

Until tonight.

She couldn't speak to him and pretend everything was all right. She couldn't pretend that she was still a princess. She had a lot of thinking to do and she couldn't burden Jasmine any further in the decisions she'd have to make about her future.

Thoughts of Juan Carlos always squeezed her heart tight in a loving embrace.

This time, though, it was as if her heart was being strangled.

And the pain of losing Juan Carlos wouldn't go away anytime soon.

Portia sat in the throne room at the palace in Del Sol, her eyes closed, her heart pumping hard. Yesterday, she'd texted and emailed Juan Carlos one excuse after another as to why she wasn't answering his calls until she'd realized the only way to break it off with him was to face him in person. She'd flown half the night to get here. To see him one last time.

His family had been through a great deal to once and for all return the true and rightful heir to the Alma throne.

There'd been one debacle after another with his cousins, as they attempted to reinstate the monarchy, and the entire process had come under great scrutiny. All eyes were on Juan Carlos now and he'd made promises, staunch, determined promises to the citizenry that he would take his role seriously. By royal decree from decades ago, he was obligated to marry a woman of royal stature. The last thing he needed was to be made a fool of by marrying an imposter, a woman who hadn't a drop of royal blood flowing through her veins.

She wasn't his perfect princess any longer.

A tear dripped down her cheek. She wiped it away and steadied her shaky breathing. She glanced down at the engagement ring she wore. It was magnificent and maybe someday would belong to a woman worthy of wearing it and claiming a place beside Juan Carlos.

Her stomach ached at the notion of Juan Carlos living with and loving another woman. But it would happen one day. Rightfully so. She could only hope getting over him wouldn't destroy her.

She heard footsteps approaching along the corridor. She rose from her seat and mustered her courage. She'd never been much of an actress, but today she needed to provide an award-winning performance.

The door opened and there he stood, dressed in a crisp white shirt, sleeves rolled up—as if he'd been busy at work—and tucked into well-fitting black trousers. A lock of his neatly combed hair swept across his forehead and his tanned face showed a hint of stubble. Some days, when he wasn't going out in public, he didn't shave. She preferred him that way...a little rough around the edges. Tall, elegant, gorgeous.

Juan Carlos's gaze lit upon her and her heart tumbled. Oh, how she'd missed him.

"Portia, sweetheart. You're here." His warm winning

smile devastated her as he strode across the room. Genuine love entered his eyes. "I'm so glad to see you. You've come back to me early."

"Yes."

"I was worried when I couldn't reach you. But now I see, you wanted to surprise me."

He took her into his arms and heaven help her, she allowed him to kiss her.

His lips were warm, welcoming, filled with passion and beautifully familiar. She'd never been kissed the way Juan Carlos kissed her. She held her back stiff and didn't partake, but he was too caught up in the moment to notice her reluctance.

"We have much to talk about," he murmured, brushing his lips over hers again.

She stepped back and gazed into his dark gleaming eyes. "Yes, Juan Carlos. It's the reason I've come back to Del Sol so quickly."

He took her hand, covering it with his. "Come, let's sit then and catch up."

He began walking, tugging her along to the king and queen's thrones, two ornate tall chairs of plush red velvet and gilded carvings.

The irony of sitting upon that chair was too much. "I'd rather stand," she said.

"Okay." He looked at her oddly, but then nodded. "Would you like to take a walk? It might feel good to stretch your legs after the long plane ride. We can talk of the progress you've made with our wedding."

"No," she said. "No, Juan Carlos. I didn't come here early to discuss our wedding. I came to say that I can't go through with it."

"With what, sweetheart?" He blinked and appeared totally confused.

"The wedding. I can't marry you, Juan Carlos. I went home and really gave our situation some thought."

"Our situation?" He frowned. "You love me, I love you. That's our situation. We're engaged, Portia."

"No, as of today, we are not."

She inhaled and twisted the diamond ring off her finger. He was shaking his head, baffled. The gleam in his eyes dimmed. He almost appeared frightened. It killed her to wipe the joy from his face. "I'm terribly sorry."

"What is all this, Portia?"

She took his hand, spread open his palm and dropped his mother's wedding ring inside. "It's too much, Juan Carlos. We…we got caught up in the moment. Finding the art treasures put us both on a crazy romantic high and we took the little fling we had too far."

"Little fling?" he repeated, his voice hitching.

Oh, God, she'd hurt him. She knew she would, but she almost couldn't bear seeing that expression on his face. Better a small lie to save him, than the truth, which would make him look the fool in the eyes of his family and country. She loved him enough to suffer his anger and wrath. But the pain she'd inflicted would stay with her a long, long time.

"It happened so fast. You and I, we're different people. I love my job, Juan Carlos."

"You wouldn't have to give it up."

"Please understand," she said softly. "It isn't going to work out. I don't want to live here. I don't want to get married or have children right now."

His eyes snapped to hers. "I never rushed you about children, Portia."

"You'd expect it one day. And…and I'm afraid I'd disappoint you. I—I… It was a mistake to get engaged."

She backed up a step, putting distance between them. God should strike her dead for the lies she was telling. But it had to be done. Her sacrifice would make it easier on Juan Carlos in the long run. Yet her heart burned at the thought of leaving him forever.

"You're having cold feet. I hear it's common before a wedding."

"No, being away from here, from you, made it all clear to me, Juan Carlos. It's not cold feet, it's reality. I hope you'll understand and not make this harder on me than it already is."

He opened his palm to stare at the diamond ring. Then the sound of his deep wobbly sigh reached her ears. He was in pain. God, she hated this. "I love you, Portia," he said, searching her eyes.

Tears blurred her vision. Her throat constricted. She couldn't return his love. For his sake, she said nothing.

He gripped her forearms, gently shaking her. As if the impact would somehow clear her head of this nonsense. "Portia, you told me you loved me. You agreed to be my wife."

"I'm...I'm..." She took a swallow. Could she do this? Could she tell the biggest lie of all? She forced the words out. "I'm fond of you, Juan Carlos."

He dropped her arms. "Fond?"

She nodded.

"Then why are you crying, sweetheart?"

Her tears now were soaking her dress. She hated herself at the moment. "I don't like hurting you."

"Then don't. Stay and we'll talk this over. Give us time, Portia."

"I can't, Juan Carlos. It won't do any good. We're... over." She sobbed now, unable to hold back any longer. "I'm s-sorry."

He didn't reach for her. Thank goodness. If he touched her again, she'd melt into his arms. But he watched her carefully, as if trying to figure her out. Skepticism lingered in his eyes. He didn't believe her, but there was also resignation there and definite injury. She must have baffled him. He didn't know what to say to convince her she was wrong.

There wasn't anything he could say to her to change her mind. This was the hardest thing she'd ever had to do. She had to leave, to muster her strength and walk out the door. "I'll never forget the time I had with you... It was... *amazing*," she whispered.

He closed his eyes, shaking his head.

And that was her way out.

She turned her back on him and dashed away, leaving the palace and Juan Carlos and the love they'd shared behind.

Nine

"If you don't mind me saying so, Your Highness, you could use some sleep. Why not close your eyes while we travel," Eduardo said.

Juan Carlos sat facing his bodyguard in the reclining lounge chair on the palace's private plane. Under normal circumstances, Juan Carlos wouldn't travel so extravagantly; he wanted to be known as the king who flew coach. But it was imperative that this journey be kept secret and away from curious eyes. "Are you saying I look less than kingly, Eduardo?"

His bodyguard straightened in his seat. "No, I, uh, I know how hard this week has been on you, Your Highness."

"Eduardo, I'm in total agreement with you." Juan Carlos sighed. "I know I look like hell. I will fix that before we arrive in Los Angeles. The best I can, that is."

Eduardo's eyes softened. "Yes, Your Majesty."

Eduardo was quickly becoming his good friend and confidant. "Do you have a girl, Eduardo?"

"Yes, I do."

"Is it serious?"

Eduardo shook his head. "No, not really."

"Because of what you do for a living?"

"Yes. I cannot get serious with anyone while I'm away so much of the time. She understands."

"Ah, an understanding woman. It's lucky for me, not so fortunate for your girl."

"*Si*, that is true. But I am twenty-eight and not ready to settle down."

"I used to think that way. But sometimes fate steps in and knocks you over the head when a beautiful snow queen enters your path."

Eduardo chuckled. "Princess Portia."

"Yes, Princess Portia. And now I'm chasing her all over the globe."

"She is worth it, I would say, Your Majesty."

"*Si*, she is worth it."

He lifted the tumbler of bourbon he held in his hand and stared into the golden liquid. "I wish you could share a drink with me, Eduardo. We'll be in the air for five more hours. Surely the effects will have worn off by then."

"Thank you, Your Majesty, but no. I cannot drink while on duty."

Juan Carlos nodded. "Coffee then and a pastry?"

"I'd never refuse a pastry from Chef Andre, Your Highness. He showed me his creations before packing them up for this trip."

Juan Carlos pressed the button on the arm of his chair and ordered up coffee and pastries from his personal flight attendant. Then he rested back in his seat and sipped bourbon. Sleep was elusive lately and eating had become a chore. But he could tolerate a shot or two of bourbon when his mind wouldn't shut down. It helped blur the pain of losing Portia.

It had been one solid week since she'd left Alma and he hadn't heard from her since. What was she doing? Had she gone back to her work routine as if *they* hadn't happened? As if the time they'd shared together was nothing more than a passing fling?

He couldn't believe that. Something was up with her.

He felt it deep down in his soul that something had happened to Portia to make her deny their love and break off their engagement. Juan Carlos had waited patiently all week to hear from her, anticipating a call that had never come, and his patience was at an end. Now he was taking matters into his own hands. He knew enough about relationships to know women liked to be pursued. They liked to have men come after them. Maybe Portia was testing him? Maybe she'd expected him to come running and convince her she'd been wrong?

If only it would be that easy.

But he had to try.

Outside of his bodyguards, he hadn't told a soul of their breakup. He couldn't bring himself to share the news so soon after publicly announcing their happy engagement. He had hopes of winning Portia back, hopes of restoring their love. He'd vowed to bring honor and credibility back to the monarchy of Alma as well as to carry out his grandmother Isabella's dying wishes for the country. He wanted, needed Portia by his side. He and Portia belonged together. She was the love of his life.

Living without her would only be half a life.

Hours later, the plane touched down in Los Angeles, a place Juan Carlos had visited often. But this time, he had more than business to attend to—he had come to retrieve his woman. He'd managed to get a few winks of sleep, shaved and changed his crumpled clothes while they were in the air. Now he felt human again and more like himself, rather than the shell of the man he'd been this past week. Dressed in a slate-gray suit and neatly groomed, he planned on sweeping his princess off her feet again.

Returning home without her wasn't an option.

"Are you ready, Your Highness?" Eduardo asked, rising from his seat.

"Yes, and you have our little surprise all set?" he asked.

"I do. If it doesn't help your cause," Eduardo said, grinning, "nothing will."

Juan Carlos nodded. He couldn't disagree.

A frozen waffle popped up out of the toaster and Portia set it next to the scrambled eggs on her plate. She doused the waffle with maple syrup, grabbed a fork and took the plate over to the kitchen table. Breakfast for dinner was always an option when one didn't have the stomach to really cook. Or eat for that matter. Her belly squeezed tight as she looked at the food. She'd promised Jasmine she would eat something tonight.

Her friend had apologized profusely for breaking their dinner date. Jas had planned to cook a roast prime rib tonight, her specialty. They were going to do it up right with champagne and soufflé, and have a fun girls' night watching Turner Classic Movies on television. It was the only reason Portia had put on a dress, instead of wearing her usual comfy gray sweats. She didn't want to disappoint her friend.

"Poor Jas." She'd come down with a bug. Hopefully it wasn't the flu. Portia felt a little guilty about it, having dominated a lot of her time lately. Jasmine had been the best friend she could ever hope to have. Every day she'd come over to help Portia clean out her closets or rearrange furniture or cook a meal. Jasmine would bring in Mexican food on Taco Tuesdays and play card games with her until very late at night. She understood Portia needed to kill time so she didn't have to think too hard.

Now her friend was sick.

"For you, Jas, I'm going to eat this." She took a bite of her eggs and chewed and chewed. The eggs went down like rubber. She'd overcooked them again.

The waffle wasn't much better. It was still frozen in the center. Two bites later, she figured she'd fulfilled her promise and took her dish to the sink, dumping the contents down the garbage disposal.

Now what? She glanced around the condo. It was spotless. She'd been cleaning all week long. She had no official work to do. She hadn't been back to the office yet—they weren't expecting her anyway since she'd taken a three-month leave to deal with wedding plans and her new life as wife to a king.

She'd truly questioned whether to go back to her job. Could she continue with the pretense? How could she go back, when her friends and associates still believed her to be Princess Portia of Samforstand? Could she go about her life, living the lie? And what if she decided it was impossible to resume her life as usual? What if she revealed all the lies about herself and her family? What would that mean for Juan Carlos? His humiliation would be monumental. He would hate her. And appear a fool, a man easily duped.

She was at a crossroads in her life, and didn't know which way to proceed.

No one could possibly know how she felt right now. She was a phony, a fraud and an imposter. Jasmine kept telling her it wasn't her fault and no one would blame her if the truth got out. But Portia didn't know who she was anymore. Her life had been ripped out from under her. She felt at odds, lonely and bereft. Her emotions were all over the place. Anger took up residence, but sympathy crept in sometimes, as she imagined her family's plight after the war. Still, those emotions didn't come close to the emptiness she felt deep inside her heart. Because of something that had happened decades ago, she had had to give up the man she loved. The price was high, costing her her happiness.

The doorbell chimed and she jumped. "Who could that be?" she whispered. Surely, Jasmine wouldn't come out tonight. She was in bed with a fever.

Portia had a mind not to open the door, but the bell chimed once again and her curiosity had her heading to the front door.

She stuck her face up to the peephole and gazed out.

"Eduardo?" What on earth was he doing here?

"*Si*, Princess, it's me."

She cringed at his reverent greeting. She didn't deserve to be called Princess. The chain lock allowed her to open the door three inches. She peered out and he smiled wide. "Hello."

Eduardo had become her friend. Seeing this solid block of a man on her doorstep was a welcome sight.

"Hi."

"Will you open the door for me?"

"Oh…of course." She undid the chain and opened the door.

Eduardo stood rooted to the spot. "Are you alone, Princess?"

"Yes, I am alone. Why?"

"I had to ask as it is my duty to protect the king. It's good to see you, but I am here on official bus—"

Juan Carlos stepped into her line of vision from a place on the porch that had concealed him. "Thank you, Eduardo. I'll take it from here."

Portia's mouth dropped open. She blinked and started trembling. "Juan Carlos."

He held a cat carrier in his hand. "Before you say anything, I brought you a gift. Well, two gifts. May I come in?"

With a lump in her throat, she looked away from Juan Carlos's face to the two kittens from Duchess's litter she'd appropriately named Mischief and Mallow. The kittens—one black and gray and mostly all trouble and the other almost all white with spots of caramel color here and there looking like a toasted marshmallow—were sleeping, curled up into little balls of fluff. Mallow's head rested on Mischief's body. Their sweetness brought a tear to her eye.

"Juan Carlos, you...you brought them," she said, touched by the thoughtful gesture. Words she wanted to say tightened in her throat and wouldn't come out. Initially, her heart had lurched when she spotted Juan Carlos, though he looked worn out. His eyes were rimmed with red—from sleepless nights? His handsome face looked haggard, as if he'd been through a war and his hair, while combed, needed a cut. She should have known he wouldn't take no very easily. He wasn't a man easily dissuaded. It was one of the qualities she loved most about him. "You didn't need to do that," she said, finally realizing she wasn't up to caring for pets. She'd barely been able to care for herself lately.

"I figured you might like the company. They are yours as much as they are mine."

She gazed into his solemn eyes. "Come in," she said.

She'd been engaged to a man who had never stepped foot into her home. How telling was that? An impetuous engagement, even though love was involved, wasn't an ideal way to start a relationship. She understood that now. During the coronation and then while living at the farmhouse searching for hidden treasures, they'd lived in a fantasy world, untouched by outside influences. It wasn't reality.

Juan Carlos stepped inside and glanced around, taking in the details of her home. "It's as beautiful as you are, Portia. I wouldn't expect any less."

"Thank you," she said. Her heart thumped hard in her chest. Thankfully, Eduardo's presence helped defuse the situation at the moment. She peered over Juan Carlos's shoulder. "Eduardo, would you like to come inside?"

She'd spent enough time with Juan Carlos and his bodyguards to know what Eduardo's answer had to be. He would be securing the premises and standing watch outside. "I wish I could, Your Highness," he said. "Thank you, but I will be right out here."

It was just as she'd suspected. "Okay, I understand." She turned to Juan Carlos and pasted on a false smile. "Surely, you and I both know that bringing me the kittens wasn't the reason you've come."

"But you're glad I did?"

She glanced at the sleeping kittens. "I'm glad to see them. They are sweet and I did...miss them." She cleared her throat. She couldn't admit she'd missed Juan Carlos also. "They've been weaned from Duchess, I'm assuming?"

He nodded. "Early this week. Where shall I put them?"

"A good question. If you'd called and asked me I would've told you not to bring them, Juan Carlos," she said softly. "I'm not equipped to care for them."

"I'll take them back to Alma with me, if you prefer." His back stiffened a little.

"No, no. Now that they're here, I can't turn them away. I... They're special to me."

Juan Carlos set the cat carrier down on the floor of the foyer. When he returned his gaze to hers, his eyes bored into her. "I had hoped you would say the same of me, sweetheart."

Her eyes closed at his hopeful plea. "You shouldn't have come, Juan Carlos."

"I couldn't stay away. It's not finished between us."

She sighed. "It has to be. We're not right for each other."

He approached her and heaven save her, her pulse accelerated as he laid his palm on her cheek. She lifted her eyes to his. His heavy expression softened, as if touching her made all the difference. As if a light inside him was turned back on. "Not true. We're good together. We're meant for each other. I am here. Don't turn me away, Portia. I would hope I am special to you, as well."

His gaze dipped to her mouth. She swallowed. Oh, God, the pull, the magnetic force of his love surrounded her like a protective shield. She didn't know where she found the will to back up a step, and then another. She couldn't hide her emotions or the passion he instilled and as she moved, he moved with her, thrusting his body against hers until her backside met with the wall.

"I've come a long way for you, Portia." His hands braced the wall, trapping her, so that she could only stare into his face and see his truth. "I've waited my entire life."

His sweet, sincere words stymied any defenses she could muster. She put her hands on his chest but instead of shoving him away as she'd planned, her fingertips clung onto his shirt and her palms flattened against him. His breath hitched from her touch, and his immediate reaction to her nearly buckled her knees. How could she not love this man? How could she turn him away now?

"I came here to talk to you, sweetheart."

She whispered, "Is that what you're doing to me? Talking?"

He flashed a charming, inescapable smile. "Maybe showing is better than telling, after all."

Then his mouth swooped over hers and claimed her in a breath-stealing kiss. His lips were rough but not unkind, wild but not crazy, sexy but not demanding. Caught up in the kiss, she couldn't think beyond the pleasure he evoked. The love she'd tried to bury was resurrected and she fell deeper in love with this man, this honorable king who had come for her.

She'd missed him and didn't know how much until this very second.

His tongue played over her lips and she opened for him. Sweeping inside her mouth, he kissed her again and again. A fire was building in her belly. She was past the point of refusal.

She was putty. He could do with her what he liked.

And she would enjoy every second.

She was lifted, floating on air now, held by two strong arms. She wrapped herself around his body, nestling her head into his chest. "Where's your bed, Portia?"

She pointed to the doorway down the hall.

His strides were long and determined and steady.

He continued to kiss her without missing a step.

Juan Carlos set Portia down on a ruffled lavender bedspread. Matching pillows, some big, some small, surrounded her head. He did a quick scan of her room decorated in soft whimsical colors. Wispy white curtains covered the windows and modern pieces of art, mostly pastels and some oils, adorned the walls. It was so Portia: soft, delicate, sweet.

God, he loved her.

And he wasn't going to leave here without her.

She was his prize, his love, the treasure he couldn't live without.

He unbuttoned his shirt, spread it wide across his chest and then gave it a toss. He kicked off his shoes and socks and gazed into her eyes as he unfastened his belt.

Her brows lifted, her lips parted slightly and a sharp breathy gasp escaped her lips. Her hungry expression softened his heart, but made every other part of his body hard. He had one night to change her mind. He wouldn't waste a minute. He took her hand and lifted her to her knees. "Come here, sweetheart," he demanded. "Touch me. Put your hands on my body."

Another gasp ripped from her lips and she moved to him. She wore a simple black dress with thin straps and short hemline. It adorned her breasts with just enough material to tempt him beyond belief. He ached to touch her, to shed her clothes and join their bodies, but first, he had to make her see how much she needed him, too. How perfect he was for her.

Her hands came to his torso and he gritted his teeth. She explored the breadth of him, tracing her fingertips over his chest, and then kissed everywhere her fingers had just touched. His body flamed; it was almost too much to bear. She was proving to him that they belonged together.

"Your touch is like no other, Portia. You know that. See what you do to me."

"We are good here, in bed, Juan Carlos," she whispered.

"We are good everywhere, sweetheart. Why do you fight me on this?"

She turned her face from him and disengaged, and he knew he'd pushed her too far. Something was eating at her. Something was making her hold back from him. "Don't retreat," he whispered. He couldn't let her think. Couldn't let whatever notions she had in her head continue to separate them.

He sank down on the bed beside her and unleashed his love for her, stripping down her defenses, loving her with everything he had inside. Holding her steady with one hand, he eased her dress off with the other, baring her upper body. He cupped her breasts, made love to them with his mouth and tongue and was rewarded with sighs of pleasure, little throaty moans of delight. Her throat, her chin, her lips. He devoured them all while covering her body with his. She arched her hips and they moved in the same unique rhythm, thrusting, aching, groaning until he couldn't take another second. He joined their bodies, pushing through her mental defenses and bringing them skin to skin.

Her eyes closed to the pleasure, her face beautifully masked in satisfaction. He thrust into her deep and long. It was hot and damp and sweaty and when he sensed her readiness, he called her name. "Portia." Her eyes snapped open. He stared into them and announced, "This is our place."

Connected by more than their bodies, she sighed and nodded her head.

Then he brought her home.

* * *

Early dawn broke through the curtains and Juan Carlos smiled in his drowsy state, his eyes still closed as images of making love to Portia flashed in his head. God, how he'd missed her. And now she was where she belonged. With him. After the night they'd shared, he hoped he'd convinced her that she loved him, he loved her and whatever was bothering her could be worked out and put to rest. It wasn't rocket science. Perhaps he'd pushed her too far early in their relationship. They'd only known each other for weeks. Not the months or years some take to cement their connection. She'd gotten cold feet. Any problems that arose could be dealt with. He couldn't see a reason why they shouldn't live their lives together. They'd made love twice during the night, and the second time had been even more thrilling and revelatory than the first. No one could tell him that Portia didn't love him. She'd displayed that in the way she'd taken the initiative, kissed him, touched him and made love to his body.

It was good, so good, between them. In all ways.

Juan Carlos rolled over to cradle her in his arms. They'd welcome the day together. But his hands hit upon cold sheets. He squeezed his eyes open. Portia was gone, her half of the bed empty. Was she always an early riser? He didn't know. They'd spent time together at the farmhouse in Alma on his schedule, not hers. There were still things they needed to learn about each other.

He hinged his body up, eager to see her. Eager to kiss her. Rising from the bed, he dressed in his trousers and shirt, ran a hand through his hair to comb down the spiky ends and then padded out of the room.

Halfway down the hallway of her modest three-bedroom condo, he halted, hearing mewling sounds coming from the living room. Of course, the kittens. Portia must have been anxious to see them this morning and tend to them the way she always had. Their carrier came equipped with kitty food, and water was their drink of choice. He grinned. He could almost picture her playing with them on the carpeted floor. Bringing them here had been a good plan to get his foot in the door and soften Portia's heart, but ultimately he'd done it to bring a smile to her face.

As he approached the sounds grew louder and no, they didn't appear to be coming from the kittens. It was a human sound, the heartbreaking echo of quiet crying. He stood on the threshold of the living room to find Portia, sitting up on the sofa, her arms around her legs, rocking back and forth with tears soaking her face.

The kittens were happily swatting at her feet, but it was as if they weren't there. Her sorrow was so deep she didn't hear him stride into the room. "Portia, sweetheart. What's wrong?"

She wiped her cheeks with the back of her hand, shaking her head. "You shouldn't have come, Juan Carlos," she whispered.

He narrowed his eyes. What on earth? Last night, they'd settled things. Maybe not verbally, but after the night they'd shared she had to recognize what they meant to each other. He'd come to retrieve her and bring her back to her rightful place, beside him on the throne of Alma. But now she was crying, looking so achingly sad. His gut clenched seeing her that way. "I don't understand."

He sat beside her and she unraveled her legs to face him, her eyes swollen from tears. "I can't be with you. I can't..."

"Sweetheart, my perfect princess, of course you belong with me. We don't have to rush into a wedding, if that's your concern. Whatever it is, we'll work it out. Just tell me. It kills me to see you in so much pain."

She rose then, yet her body slumped in defeat, her long hair falling onto her face. "That's just it, Juan Carlos," she said, shoving her hair aside. "I'm not your perfect princess.

I'm nobody's princess. I'm a fraud. I don't have an ounce of royal blood in my body. I cannot marry you. Ever."

Juan Carlos blinked several times, absorbing her words. He rose slowly, his heart pounding, his body shaking. "What you do mean you're not a princess?"

"I'm not. I never was. It's all a lie my family told after they migrated to the United States after World War II."

Portia spent the next few minutes explaining her family's duplicity to him. She gave him very little to hold on to as she presented the cold cruel facts that tore his life into shreds. Everything she told him made sense, yet nothing made sense. This couldn't be happening. Suddenly, he looked at Portia Lindstrom differently. She'd lied to him. Why? "How long have you known this?"

"I found out a little more than a week ago while researching our…my wedding rituals."

Juan Carlos stood ramrod stiff, his shoulders back and his heart breaking. "Yet you came to me and lied about the reasons for breaking it off between us. You told me you weren't ready to marry. You gave me excuses about your career and your love of the States. You knew, and yet you lied. How many other lies have you told me, Portia?"

"I didn't know what to do when I found out. Who to turn to. I'd just found out I'm…I'm an *imposter*." She spit the word out as if saying it stung her tongue. "I had trouble facing it, Juan Carlos."

His voice rose. "You should have trusted me with the truth. Or maybe you didn't want anyone to know the real truth? Maybe you wanted to keep on with the deception? Being of royal blood has its privileges. If I hadn't shown up here, what were you going to do? Live the lie forever?"

Her words from last week rang in his ears. *I'm fond of you. This isn't going to work. I don't want to get married. I don't want children.*

Had the woman he loved been nothing but a gold dig-

ger? Had her hard-to-get act been a ploy? All the warmth
he had nestled inside evaporated. Last night had meant
nothing to her. She'd deceived him over and over during
the past few weeks. She'd broken off her engagement to
him, but she hadn't revealed the truth to anyone. Of course,
her precious career would suffer. She'd hidden the truth because she couldn't afford another scandal. She needed the
art world to believe that she was a princess. So, of course,
she had to come to him with lies about why she was breaking off their engagement in order to keep her secret.

"I took the bait and you reeled me in, didn't you, Portia? Then what happened? You ran scared when I offered
marriage? Did you have a bout of conscience? Or did you
finally realize you'd get caught if you didn't break it off
with me? You couldn't marry me and risk being found out.
Just think what would happen to your career if you were
discovered to be a fraud. You'd never survive another scandal. Not professionally. No one in their right mind would
hire you so you lied your way out of our engagement."

Her tears gone now, she squeezed her eyes closed for a
second. As he waited, her breathing steadied and when she
opened her eyes again, they were twin pinpoints of blue,
focused on him. "You see things in black-and-white, Juan
Carlos. There is no room for grays in your narrow line of
vision. You only wanted me when I fit into your plans,
but now you know the truth. I'm not royal. I'm flawed and
can't be a part of your unblemished world."

His lips tightened. "You should've told me the truth,
Portia."

"Another point against me. I'm human. I make mistakes." She folded her arms across her stomach. "Now
that you have the truth, what are you going to do with it?"

He stared at her, wondering what had happened to the
woman he'd fallen in love with. Thoughts clogged his head.
She wasn't a princess. She had no royal blood flowing

through her veins. She was an imposter. A fraud, as she put it. His shoulders dropped as he shook his head. He had no answer for her.

"You only loved the idea of me, Juan Carlos. You said it just a little while ago. You think of me as your perfect princess. But now you know I'm not perfect. Hardly that. And how can a man who demands perfection in everything and everyone want me? I was only good to you when I was Princess Portia of Samforstand."

He let that sink in. He loved her, wanted her as his wife. Now, nothing made sense, and blackness from deep in his soul overwhelmed him. His Portia, the woman he'd thought she was, was gone. She wasn't a princess, but a fraud. He couldn't marry Portia Lindstrom. According to royal decree he was obligated to marry royalty. She was once a part of everything good that had happened to him and now there was nothing left between them.

"We had a fling, and it's over," she whispered. "Let's let it go at that. I think you should leave. Go back to Del Sol, be the king you were meant to be. Give me some time, I'll make sure...no blame will come to you about this."

"Portia," he said. He couldn't bring himself to move.

"Go, please." Her quiet plea broke his heart. "You shouldn't have come back. Goodbye, Juan Carlos."

She picked up the kittens playing at her feet, hugged them to her chest and walked out of the room.

She was right. He should leave.

There wasn't anything left for him here.

"Mr. Tanaka, it was a pleasure seeing you again. I'll be in touch once I've found the right prints and antique paneled floor screens to separate your work spaces. You've given me a good idea what you are looking for. I promise you, you'll be happy with the collection I come up with for your magnificent new corporate offices."

"Thank you, Princess. I have faith in your abilities. Your recommendations for my home have worked out nicely. I'm grateful you would take time from your leave of absence to do this for me."

Portia shook hands with her client outside his private office, her belly squeezing tight every time he called her princess. The title she'd grown up with no longer rang true and his respectful use of it during their meeting reminded her constantly that she was a fraud. "Goodbye."

Mr. Tanaka, founder and president of a highly successful Japanese food chain, hadn't wanted to work with anyone else. He'd called her personally to request her expertise, offering a big bonus if she would consider advising him on the artwork for his new offices. She'd agreed without hesitation. Pining for Juan Carlos and what would never be had grown old. She couldn't cry herself to sleep any longer. Three days' worth of tears had exhausted her. But she was glad her secret was out. At least to him. Admitting the truth to Juan Carlos had been difficult, but it had also been liberating. There would be no more lies between them now.

He'd been angry with her when he'd left her condo the other day. She'd seen the pain in his eyes, too, and she'd shivered when he'd looked at her as if she were a stranger. It had been so very hard to hear him berate her. He hadn't believed her, and even thought so little of her that he'd accused her of putting her career above her love for him. His accusations had slashed through her body like a dagger. But ultimately, it was better to allow him to believe the worst about her. It was a clean break.

Still, the love she had for him would never die. It would be hard, if not impossible, to get over him. Even if he had believed her claims, he couldn't marry her. They would have no future. He lived by a stringent set of rules. He did everything by the book. It was a no-win situation. So she'd made the supreme sacrifice for his benefit. She'd dismissed him without defending herself. As if her life wouldn't be forever altered after knowing and loving him.

He would get over her. He had to. He had to go about his life as if they had never met. In the near future, she didn't know exactly when, she would quietly make an announcement that they'd broken off their engagement. Their whirlwind romance was over. And then at some later point, when it had all died down, she would admit to the world, or anyone who cared, that she wasn't of royal heritage.

She would not go on living a lie.

But for now her goal was to protect Juan Carlos from a scandal. She would not have him looked upon as a fool.

As she headed to the parking garage, her eyes clouded with tears. She was broken inside and there was no way to repair her. Taking on Mr. Tanaka's account would be a good distraction. She'd focus on work for the next few weeks and the terrible ache in the pit of her stomach would eventually go away.

She got in her car and glanced in the mirror. She looked a wreck. With the tips of her index fingers, she smoothed away moisture under her eyes. "No more," she whispered. She had to put on a happy face. It was Jasmine's birthday today and she was taking her to dinner to celebrate the big three-oh.

Ten

Juan Carlos ran a hand down his face. He stood at the bar in the study of his living quarters in the palace and poured himself a double whiskey, straight up. "It's impossible." He lifted the glass to his mouth and took a sip.

"What's impossible?"

He turned, a little shocked to find Maria standing beside him. He'd been so deep in thought, he'd almost forgotten about his dinner date with the Ramons tonight. Normally his senses were keen and no one could sneak up on him. Especially not a woman wearing a pretty dress and heels and smelling like something exotic. It served to show him how off he'd been lately.

"Sorry if I startled you. Your staff assured me I was expected."

"No, it's okay. You are." It was good to see a friendly face.

"Alex is running late. He's meeting me here."

Juan Carlos nodded. "That'll give us a chance to talk. Let me get you a drink. What would you like?"

"Just a soda, please."

He dropped two ice cubes into a tall glass and poured her a cola. "Here you go."

She took the offered glass and sipped. "So what were you mumbling about when I came in?"

The corner of his mouth crooked up. It was the best he could do. He didn't have a smile for anyone these days. "My life."

"Your life?" Maria's aqua eyes opened wider. "Your perfect, kingly, marrying-a-beautiful-princess life?"

He lifted his whiskey glass and pointed with his index finger to the bone leather sofa. "Have a seat. I have something to... I need some advice."

Maria arched an eyebrow. "Advice? About your wedding?"

He waited for her to sit and then planted himself on the other end of the sofa. "Maria, uh, there isn't going to be a wedding."

It was hard getting the words out, and seeing Maria's mouth drop open only added to his discomfort. "That's why I asked you here. I haven't told a soul yet. I can hardly believe it myself."

"But you and Portia seemed so perfect together. What happened?"

Perfect. He was beginning to really hate that word. Portia had accused him of demanding that everyone and everything around him be perfect. Was he guilty of that? Did he expect too much?

"We're not perfect. Far from it. We've broken up and I don't know what to think about it."

"Why? What happened, Your Majesty?"

"She came back to Del Sol almost two weeks ago to break it off. She claimed she didn't want to get married and move to Alma. She loved her career and didn't want it to end. She claimed all we had was a fling, and that she, we, were high on romance. Finding the hidden artwork and being on the adventure together made it all seem possible but when she got back home, she was hit with reality."

"Do you think she was running scared?"

He hung his head, staring at the ground. "Initially, that's what I thought. I believed I could convince her that we could work out logistics and that we belonged together."

He met with Maria's eyes. "I was fool enough to go after her. I was in love."

"Was?"

He shrugged. "From the day I met her, something inside me told me she was the one. I pursued her like crazy. She didn't make it easy and now that I'm home, putting the pieces together, I think I know why."

There was a beat of silence. Maria was waiting for him to continue. It was difficult to admit to anyone how wrong he'd been. "When I went to Los Angeles, we...connected again. And it was as it had always been—amazing. I thought I'd relieved her of her cold feet. But in the morning, I found her quietly crying. She said she wished that I hadn't come for her. I was confused and didn't know why she'd had a change of heart."

"Why did she?" Maria asked.

He shrugged and shook his head. "I think she was cornered and didn't see a way out, so she finally told me the truth. Portia is not who she says she is. She's not a princess. She never was. She claims she found out while trying to dig up protocols for our wedding. Her family fled to the United States right after World War II and assumed the role of royalty. They were impoverished and used their phony status to gain a leg up. Supposedly, Portia's great-aunt has a diary that confirms all this."

"Wow, this is...big. Poor Portia. She must've been devastated when she found out. I can only imagine how she feels right now."

He stared at her. "You mean you believe that she didn't know about this all along?"

"Why wouldn't I? More importantly, why wouldn't you?"

"I'll tell you why. When she came back to Del Sol a couple weeks ago she lied about her reasons for breaking it off. She made up one excuse after another and if I hadn't gone to LA, I would still believe those lies she'd told. Only when she couldn't get rid of me any other way, she was forced to reveal the truth."

"Oh, I don't know about that." Maria began shaking her head. "That doesn't sound like Portia. What did you say to her when you found out?"

"In the beginning I was shell-shocked. And then my methodical mind started working and I said some things out of anger. I practically accused her of being a gold digger. Now that I think back on it, she looked so…lost. She kept saying she was an imposter, and I couldn't sympathize with her. I wasn't in the frame of mind. I felt betrayed. She should have come to me with the truth from the beginning."

"It must've been a hard thing for her to admit. To herself, much less to the man she loved. Just think, everything she believed about herself and her life is a lie. If that were me, I wouldn't know what to do, who to turn to. I don't know if I'd have the courage to do what she did. It was a hard day for both of you."

He drew oxygen into his lungs. "I suppose. I still don't know what to think."

"What else did she say? How did you part?"

"She pretty much told me off. She said that I expected perfection in everything and that I only loved the idea of her." He stared into his tumbler at the last gulp of whiskey left. "That's not true."

"No?"

He gave Maria a glance. "No," he assured her. "I loved her."

"You still love her, Your Majesty. You can't shut down those emotions so quickly. And what if she still is that woman you fell in love with, without the title of princess in front of her name? What if Portia Lindstrom is the woman for you?"

"How can I believe that when she doesn't believe it? She

didn't try to defend herself against my accusations. She didn't try to convince me that I'd been wrong about her."

"Well, since you asked me for my advice, I'm going to give it to you. I know Portia a little bit, and I'm a pretty good judge of character. I have seen the way she looks at you. The eyes don't lie. She was deeply in love and happy."

A lump formed in his throat. In the short weeks that he and Portia had been together, they'd gotten to know each other pretty well. They'd shared an adventure or two, but it went deeper than that and he'd felt they were meant for each other from the very beginning. It was a sense he had, a feeling that clamped onto him and never let go. It wasn't an overreaction to her beauty or the fact that she was a princess. But that factored into the equation, at least a little bit, because her status meant he was free to seriously pursue her.

"I thought so, too," he said. "We were good together."

"Did you ever stop to think that she wasn't thinking about herself when she broke up with you? Maybe she loved you so much she didn't want you portrayed in a bad light. A hasty then broken engagement wouldn't instill much faith in the monarchy you are trying to reestablish. After the big splash announcing your engagement, how would King Juan Carlos appear to the country that trusted his honor? Wouldn't it make you seem frivolous? Or duped? Or worse yet, impetuous? Seems to me, if I was in that situation, I would do everything in my power to protect the man I loved from scorn and speculation."

He scrubbed his jaw and sighed. "The last thing she told me was that she would make sure no blame came to rest on my shoulders."

Maria smiled. "There, you see. Only a woman still in love would say that. She was shielding you from harm. I would bet on it."

"You would?"

"Yes, and you should, too, if you still love her."

"To what end? I can't change the future…"

"Who says you can't? You're the king."

"I'm not that kind of king. I don't want to break with tradition."

"No, you'd rather have your heart broken."

Juan Carlos sighed. She was right. He would never love another the way he loved Portia. Right now, he physically ached for her.

Maria continued, "Think of it this way. You'll rule with more clarity and fairness having Portia by your side. You won't be stung by bitterness and regret and live an empty life without her."

"But the people expect—"

"A ruler they can admire and look up to. If you make it clear to them that this is for the best, they will rally behind you, my friend. And as the newly reigning king of a lost monarchy you have the luxury of not needing a parliament to vote on changes you might want to make in your dynasty."

A slow smile spread across his face. "I hadn't thought of that." And just as the notion elevated his hope, another thought brought him down again. "No…it's too late after the way I walked out on Portia, without believing in her. She may not forgive me."

Maria scooted closer to him, the sparkle in her eyes grabbing his attention. "But she may. And I think she will. She sacrificed herself for you. Don't you think you owe your relationship one more chance? If you don't try, you'll always wonder and you'll live to regret it."

Did he still love Portia? Yes, very much, and the more he thought about Maria's argument, the more he began to believe she could be right. He couldn't throw away something so precious to him without giving it one more try.

A light flashed in his head as he began to formulate a

plan. Finally, after these past few days of living in a depressed stupor, he was waking up alert and seeing things much more clearly. He had the power of the throne behind him. He hoped it would be enough.

"Maria, I'm going to need your help."

"I'll give it gladly, Your Highness."

A knot formed in the pit of his stomach. "A lot will be riding on this," he warned.

"I know. But I have enough faith in love for both of us. Alex says I've taught him something about that."

Juan Carlos nodded. If only he had that same faith. He leaned forward to kiss Maria's cheek. "Thank you."

"What is it exactly that you've taught me, sweetheart?" Alex stood at the threshold of the study, catching Juan Carlos's lips leaving Maria's cheek.

"How important *trust* is, Alex," Maria said slowly, straightening her position on the sofa, "when it comes to matters of the heart."

Alex gave them a nod as he entered the room. "It's true…once upon a time my fist might've met with His Majesty's jaw seeing him kiss you. But now, I only see love shining in your eyes for me."

A chuckle rumbled from Juan Carlos's chest. It was a good sound. One he hoped to make more often, after Portia was back where she belonged.

The sound of her Nikes pounding against the treadmill echoed off the gym walls. Sweat beaded up on Portia's forehead as she gazed out the window of the high-rise. She was offered a view of distant mountains and below, a city waking just after dawn. It was a good time of day to work out, before the world came alive. She had about thirty minutes before the gym would crowd with businessmen and women coming for their daily fix. She'd be gone by then, away from any nosy members who'd try to talk to her, get to know her. Many people recognized her, but thankfully she was old news as the other royal couple— the Brits—were in town for a charity event and all eyes had turned to them.

It was a lucky break and she valued the bit of anonymity it afforded her.

"Oh…kay, Portia," Jasmine said, shutting down her machine. "I've had enough."

Portia continued running at a six-mile-per-hour pace. She had one more mile to go. "You've barely broken a sweat."

"You're insane this morning." Jas used her towel to wipe her face as droplets rained down from her eyebrows.

Portia slowed her pace, allowing her body to cool down. "I know. But this is the only time I have to work off my…"

"Sexual frustration."

Portia swiped at her friend's butt with her workout towel. "Shh…no. Stop that! Just frustration in general."

Jasmine reached over and pushed the Off button on Portia's machine. "You're done."

The treadmill's thrumming quieted as it shut down and Portia finally stood stationary facing Jas. "I know I am. So done." She sopped up her face and neck and allowed herself a moment of accomplishment. It had been a hearty workout.

"I meant on the machine, girl. You're being cryptic today. What's really bothering you?"

Aside from her broken heart? It was hard to put into words exactly but she tried to explain. "I'm almost finished with the Tanaka account, Jas. You've helped me so much this past week and we've been working at breakneck speed for long hours. When I'm through… I don't know how it will play out. I'm still officially on leave. I don't know what to do after this. I'm living a lie, but I can't do anything about it at the moment. I feel weird in my own skin right now."

"Wow, Portia, I'm sorry. Juan Carlos doesn't deserve you. You're hurting because of him."

"You got that backward. I don't deserve him."

"Oh, brother. Listen, I know it's going to take time getting over him, but you will, honey. I hate to stand by and see you beat yourself up over something out of your control."

"Thanks, Jas. It means a lot to know you have my back."

"I do."

They left the workout area and headed to the showers. After a quick rinse off, Portia dressed in her casual street clothes and combed her hair.

"Too bad we can't grab breakfast," Jas said, exchanging a look with Portia in the dressing room mirror as she slipped her long mane into a ponytail.

"Wish we could, but we've both got busy mornings. Sorry if I'm overworking you on this account."

"You're not at all. I was only looking for an excuse to have waffles and bacon this morning."

"And you wanted an accomplice, right?"

Jas nodded. "No fun eating alone."

"Another day, I promise."

"Okay, then I'll talk to you later. Oh, and thanks," she said, wrinkling her nose, "for dragging my butt in this morning." She pouted. "I ache all over and my legs feel like Jell-O."

"You'll thank me in twenty years when you're still hot and gorgeous."

"So I guess I'll have to be your friend forever now."

"BFFs. That's us."

"Yeah, that's us," Jas said, waving goodbye.

Portia rode the elevator down to the parking garage. Just as she was getting into her Volvo, her phone beeped. She glanced at the screen. Odd, she'd gotten a text from Maria Ramon.

I'm in town and would love to see you. Can you make time for me today?

"No," she whispered. Any reminder of Juan Carlos right now was hard to take. Seeing Maria would only bring back memories of her time in Alma. She did have a terribly busy day. Hadn't she just turned down a breakfast date with her best friend?

Another text came in. It's important that I see you.

Portia's breath caught in her throat. Her heart began to pound. She couldn't refuse Maria. She was a friend and more than that, Portia was curious as to what she wanted. But that didn't stop her hands from trembling as she typed her answer. Sure, would love to see you. Stop by this morning. She gave her the address and sighed, starting the car. She planned on working from home this morning, anyway.

As it turned out, Portia couldn't concentrate when she returned home. Those phone conversations could wait another day, she decided. She changed into a powder-blue silk blouse and white slacks, and brushed her hair back and clipped it on one side with a gemstone barrette à la Gwen Stefani. She finished with a few flips of mascara to her lashes and some pink lip gloss.

In the kitchen, she prepared coffee, arranged fresh pastries on a plate, and then brought it all to the dining table. Mischief and Mallow played at her feet, swatting none too gently at her toes. Before they destroyed her sandals, she scooped them both up and carried them to the sofa. "Here, let's cuddle," she said, laying them across her chest. They obeyed, burrowing into the warmth of her body. The sound of their purring brought a smile to her face. She stroked the top of their soft downy heads. She loved the two fur balls with all of her heart.

A few minutes later, the doorbell chimed and Portia jerked up straight. The quick move sent the kittens tumbling to the floor. The little guys landed on their feet. Oh, to be a cat.

Portia rose and glanced at herself in the foyer mirror, checking hair and makeup. She approached the door, but her hand shook on the knob. She paused, took a deep breath. *Stay calm, Portia. Maria is a friend.*

She opened the door to find Maria smiling warmly, her pretty aqua eyes bright. A sharp twinge tightened Portia's belly. "Hi, Maria."

"Portia, it's good to see you."

She stepped forward to give Maria a hug. "I'm happy to see you, too. Please come in," she said, retreating as Maria made her way into the foyer.

She glanced around, noting the high-vaulted ceilings and the living and dining rooms. "It's a lovely place, Portia."

She shrugged. "Thanks. It's a rental. I travel back and forth from coast to coast a lot, so I have a small apartment in New York City, too. I haven't really made this place my own yet." She'd never felt settled enough in either place to put too much of herself into them. Aside from her treasured artwork on the walls, the rest of her furniture was simply... there. She had no emotional attachment to it, which had never really dawned on her before now. "It's not a big place. Would you like a tour?"

"Sure." Portia walked her through the condo, showing her the home office, the guest bedroom, her master suite and the kitchen. They stopped in the dining room. "Would you like coffee and a pastry?"

Maria's eyes darted to the dish of fresh pastries. They were impressive. Portia knew the pastry chef at the Beverly Hills Hotel and she'd made a call this morning to have them delivered. "I'd love some. Thank you. It's good seeing you in your own element here. This is very nice."

"Let's have a seat," Portia said. "Everything's ready." Maria sat down across the table and Portia poured them each a cup of coffee. "I was surprised, in a good way, to hear from you this morning. What brings you to California?"

Maria cradled the cup in her hands. "I, uh, I had no real business here, Portia. I came specifically to see you."

"Me?" Portia halted before the cup touched her lips. "Why?"

"Maybe because I'm a hopeless romantic. Maybe because I found the love of my life in Alex and want my friends to find that same kind of happiness. Don't get me wrong, Portia, I'm not here to meddle, but I do think Juan Carlos made a mistake with you."

"He told you?" Portia wasn't sure how she felt about that.

"Yes, I know you've broken the engagement."

"Who else knows?"

"No one. I don't think he's told his cousins yet."

Portia nodded. Her belly began to ache. "Do you know everything?"

Maria's expression softened. "I know you're not a princess, Portia. Juan Carlos told me the entire story. I'm so sorry you were misled all those years. It must have been extremely difficult finding out the way that you did."

Portia's eyes squeezed shut at the truth of those words. "Yes." Oh, God. This was so hard. If only she could blink this entire ordeal away. Too bad life wasn't that easy. Soon everyone would know her dirty little secret and they probably wouldn't be as kind as Maria. "It's been an adjustment. My whole life is a lie."

"Not all of it, Portia."

She snapped her eyes open, just as Maria's hand came to touch hers. She welcomed the warmth of her friend's gentle touch. "I can't possibly know exactly how you feel, but I do know you. Portia Lindstrom is a wonderful, sweet, caring woman. She's smart and funny and she's terribly in love with a good man."

Portia shook her head. "No. Juan Carlos…there's nothing left between us."

"There's love, Portia. Don't discount it. It makes the world go round, you know."

"Well, I'm spinning fast, Maria. And I'm about to fall off."

"No, you don't have to fall off. I know Juan Carlos still loves you. He's made a terrible mistake. He was in shock, I think, hearing the news about your identity, and he regrets how you two left off. He's sorry for how he treated you, Portia."

"I accept his apology. If that's what you came for, you can tell him not to worry about me. I'm…fine."

"That's not why I came. You love him very much, don't you?"

Portia sat silent.

"I know you're protecting him, Portia. I know, because if I were in your shoes, I'd do the same thing."

"You would?"

"Yes. Isn't it why you initially lied about the reason you broke off your engagement?"

"Maybe."

"Maybe yes?"

"Okay, yes. That's why I lied. It was inevitable that we had to break up, so why should both of us go down with the ship? I was to blame. It was my family's illicit behavior that put us in this position. Juan Carlos didn't need to suffer, too."

"I thought so." Maria selected a pastry and eased it onto her plate. "Juan Carlos is very lucky."

Portia scoffed. "Hardly. I'm a fraud."

"No, you're not, Portia. You may not be a princess, but that's not all you are. Juan Carlos believes in your love."

"Then why isn't he here? Never mind. I'm glad he's not. It was hard enough breaking it off with him the first and second time."

Maria chewed her raspberry cheese tart with a thoughtful expression on her face. "The third time's the charm, they say. And he's not here, because well, he wants to see you again. In fact, it's urgent that he see you. But he wants you to come to Alma. What he has to say must be said in Del Sol."

"Me? Go back to Alma? I couldn't possibly."

"I was afraid you'd say that. I'm not to leave here without you, but…I think I have something that will change your mind."

"Nothing much could change my mind."

"Wait right here. I have something in my car. I'll only be thirty seconds," Maria said, rising. "Don't you think about putting those pastries away."

Portia smiled despite the mystery unfolding. What on earth was Maria up to?

Just seconds later, Maria walked back into the dining room holding a large package wrapped in brown paper. The box was the size of a small television or a microwave. Ridiculous.

"What do you have there?"

"Oh, no, I'm not telling. You have to open it. First read the note."

"I don't see a note?"

"It's inside."

Portia stared at Maria and shook her head. Nothing would get her to change her mind. But she had to admit, she was intrigued. Her eye began to twitch. *Damn. Stop it.* Okay, she was nervous.

"Go on," Maria said.

Portia dug her fingers into the wrapping and tore it away. Paper flew in all directions. An envelope with her name on it taped to the box popped into her line of vision. She lifted it off, pulled the note out and read it silently.

Portia, sweetheart,
Give me another chance to prove my love.
This was to be my wedding gift to you.
I hope you will accept it and me back into your life.
It speaks for itself.
Juan Carlos

Tears trickled down her face. The note was short, but held the words that could make all things possible. She loved Juan Carlos. Would always love him. And now, dare she take a chance? What could he have possibly sent that would impact her more than those loving words?

"Open the box, Portia."

"I'm afraid to," she said, eyeing the lid, her body shaking so badly she could hardly move. "What if it isn't…"

"It is. Trust me," Maria said.

Portia pulled open the lid and found yet another box. She lifted it out and set it on the table, staring at the ornate workmanship on the box, the beautiful wood carvings of intricate design.

She undid the latch and slowly eased the lid open. She eyed her gift and a soft gasp rose up from the depths of her throat. This was amazing. Sweet. The gesture meant more to her than anything else she could imagine. Her lips began to quiver, her heart pounded and her tears fell like heavy rain.

"It's the s-statue. My favorite p-piece of the artwork we…" She gulped and whispered, "It's from the hidden treasure we uncovered." A man reaching his hand out for the woman he loves. *"Almas Iguales. Equal Souls."*

A royal chauffeur met her at the Del Sol airport terminal, grabbing up her suitcases and guiding her toward the limousine parked just outside the entrance. She was taking a giant leap of faith coming here, offering up her heart once again. But Juan Carlos had done the one thing, given her the one gift that could change her mind. His generous gesture told her he understood her, believed in her and wanted her back in his life. She didn't see how it was possible. She didn't know what terms Juan Carlos would dictate to her when she arrived. Could she bank on his integrity? Could she trust in him enough to believe there was a solution to their dilemma?

His gift had jarred her into believing the best was yet to come. But as the hours had worn on, she'd started to doubt again. It had taken Maria and Jasmine both to convince her that if she didn't travel to Del Sol and give it one last try, she would live to regret it.

"He's been solely devoted to you since the minute he set eyes on you," Maria had said.

"Think of your time at the farmhouse," Jasmine had prodded. "How many other men would rescue feral cats and give them a good home, much less a royal palace, to make you happy? And don't forget how he battled a snake to keep you safe. He's been there for you, Portia. And he'll be there for you again."

"Go, give your love another chance," they'd both chorused.

So here she was back in Del Sol where in less than an hour, Juan Carlos would address the citizens of his country in a speech that would set the tone for his rule.

The driver opened the limo door. "Thank you." She slid inside and immediately turned, startled to find Juan Carlos in the seat beside her.

"Hello, sweetheart."

The richness in his voice seeped into her soul. She faced the most handsome man she'd ever known. His eyes were deep dark shades of coffee and cocoa, flecked with hints of gold, and he was gazing at her in that intense way that made her heart soar. His smile was warm, welcoming and filled with the confidence she lacked at the moment. Oh, how she'd missed him. A whisper broke from her lips. "Juan Carlos."

"I am glad you came."

He didn't reach for her, didn't try to touch her, and she was glad. She had to catch her breath just from seeing him. Anything more would send her into a tailspin. "I, uh, I don't know why I'm here."

He sighed. "It's because you love me."

She couldn't deny it. "Yes."

"And I love you, above all else. I have misjudged you and I am truly sorry, my love. I hope your being here means you have forgiven me."

A lump formed in her throat. How could she explain the complexities of her feelings? "I do forgive you. Though it hurt, I realized you reacted as anyone might."

"But I am not just anyone, Portia. I am the man who loves you unconditionally. And I should have recognized that sooner. I should have believed in you."

"Yes. But that wouldn't have changed the outcome. Our situation is impossible, Juan Carlos."

He only smiled. "Did you like my gift?"

Tears welled in her eyes. "It's magnificent. I was truly surprised by the gesture."

"Not a gesture, sweetheart. It's a gift from my heart to yours. And I have another gift for you. One that will make all things possible. I am only asking for your trust. Do I have it?"

She hesitated for only a moment. And in that moment, she realized that yes, she trusted him with her life. She trusted him to make the right decision. She trusted him. With. Her. Heart. She nodded.

"Good."

He took her hand and lifted it to his lips, pressing the

softest, most reverent kiss there. The sweetness of the gesture left her floating on air. "I have missed you."

Their eyes met then. His were unflappable, determined, loving. She saw everything she needed in their brown depths. Then his hands were on her, cupping her face, his thumbs stroking her cheeks as his gaze flowed over her face. She was out of her depths now, living in the moment, heat crawling up from her belly to lick at her. When his lips rained down on hers, devouring her mouth in a kiss to beat all kisses, tremendous hunger swept her up and carried her away.

His groans matched her unbridled sighs. "I cannot live without you in my life," he murmured between kisses.

"I feel the same," she whispered, as he dragged her farther into his embrace. She was nearly atop him now. His hands were in her hair, his tongue sweeping through her mouth, their bodies trembling, aching.

"We have arrived, Your Highness," the driver announced through the speaker. They'd arrived? She didn't remember them taking off.

Juan Carlos stilled. "All right," he said to the chauffeur.

They had indeed arrived at a secluded private entrance in the west wing of the palace.

Juan Carlos sighed heavily and pulled away from her. "One day, we will finish this in the limo."

"I'll look forward to that." Her eyelid fluttered. Heavens, another unintended wink? She was hopeless.

Intense heat entered his eyes and a savage groan rumbled from his chest. "You are a temptation, Portia," he said. He took a second to smooth the hair he'd just mussed. The care with which he touched her and gently pulled tendrils away from her face sent shivers down her spine. Then he smiled wide and destroyed her for good. "You will attend my speech?"

"Yes." That was why she had come. His only request

was that she be in attendance when he spoke to the press and his fellow countrymen. Her flight had been delayed and there was a moment when she'd thought it an omen. A moment when she almost turned back. But Portia wasn't going to run from the truth any longer. No matter how bad. No matter that her life would be forever altered. She had gotten on the plane ready to hear what Juan Carlos seemed eager to say. He would be giving the speech very shortly. "I will be there."

He nodded, satisfied, and the door on his side of the car opened. The driver stood at attention waiting. "You'll be driven to the palace lawn now," he said to her. "I will see you very soon."

Then he climbed out of the car and was gone.

Juan Carlos stood tall and erect at the podium looking out at the crowd that had gathered on the palace lawn. Dressed regally in a dark suit and tie, he scanned his audience. Luis and Eduardo flanked him on either side, on the lookout for signs of danger. News crews from Del Sol's three television stations were in attendance, as well as reporters and journalists from far and wide. Portia saw Juan Carlos now, as the king surrounded by people who banked on his every word. He was a model citizen, handsome, refined, a man to be admired. He was the king of his people. The press loved him. Even more, they loved the idea of him *with Portia*. Who didn't love a good fairy tale?

Her stomach ached. She had no idea what he was going to say, but it was important to him that she hear him say it. There was no doubt she loved him. And she was fairly certain of his love for her. So she stood in the front row, but off to the side somewhat with Maria and Alex Ramon. Maria slid her hand over hers and squeezed gently. God, how Portia needed that show of support right now. Her legs were two rubber posts, holding her up only by sheer stubborn will. She swallowed as Juan Carlos tapped the mike, ready to begin his speech.

And when he spoke, his voice came across clear, strong and confident. Tears of pride pooled in her eyes. He addressed the crowd, garnering cheers as he began his speech. Then he graciously spoke of the future, of how he planned to work alongside the parliament to better the country. He spoke of helping the needy, working with charities and letting the people of Alma have a voice.

He seemed to seek her out of the crowd and as those gorgeous dark eyes landed on her, her breath caught in her throat. He trained that killer smile on her once again. How unfair of him to have such power over her, to stop her breathing with a look, a smile.

All eyes in the crowd seemed to turn her way. She was no stranger to the press, to having people recognize her, but today, she wanted no such attention. She'd rather be invisible.

Maria squeezed her hand again, giving her silent support. Portia inhaled and began breathing again.

"I have one more announcement to make," he continued to his audience. "Actually it is the reason I have called you here. I have made a decision that will change the ways of the monarchy for the better, I hope. For decades past, those in power, the honorable men and women who held the highest rule of the land, often did so out of duty. But with their duty often came great sacrifice." Juan Carlos glanced at Portia again briefly and then went on. "Many true loves went unheeded. Many of those loves were lost to baseless marriages, unions that held no great affection. The sacrifice was thought to keep the bloodlines pure. I have called you here today to say that my rule, this monarchy, is one that looks forward to the future, not backward at the past. It is time to bring the monarchy into the twenty-first century.

"As you know, Portia Lindstrom and I are to be married. Our engagement was swift, yes, but when it's right, you know it deep in your heart." His fist covered his heart and he awarded the crowd his beautiful smile. "And I am here to tell you it is right."

His eyes sparkled and he sent her a look filled with so much love, Portia's heart did somersaults. "Recently, it's come to light that Portia is not the true princess of Samforstand. In fact, she has no royal bloodlines at all. She came to me when she learned this news from an elder in her family. It seems there was much confusion about the legal heirs to the throne after the chaos and hardships of World War II.

"My family went through great hardships at that time, as well. Many of you here today know all about the recent trials and tribulations my family went through to find the true heir to the throne. Our great-grandmother's recently discovered letters proved to all of us the high price that was paid to keep to the letter of law when it came to royal protocol. In those letters we learned that her son, king Raphael Montoro II, and his direct descendants were not the rightful heirs to the throne, and thus am I standing before you today, a Salazar, as your king.

"Similarly, Portia has discovered the truth of her family's past and now needs to move forward with her life. But I will not allow mere decorum to once again steer the Montoros' destiny toward a tragic outcome. We will not let history repeat itself. We will not sacrifice our love in the name of an outdated custom. Portia Lindstrom is here today, as my fiancée, and princess or not, she is the love of my life and will become my wife."

Juan Carlos put out his hand. "Portia? Will you join me here? Be by my side."

The crowd was stunned into silence. Cameras angled her way, shots were snapped off by the dozens.

"Go," Maria whispered. "He is changing a centuries-old tradition for you. Don't leave him waiting."

She blinked, coming to grips with what had just happened. The depth of his commitment astonished her, delighted her and sent her hormones into a tizzy. She caught Eduardo giving her a smile and an encouraging nod from behind Juan Carlos. She smiled back.

Maria was right; she couldn't leave the king waiting. Not for another second. If he could do this for her, then she wouldn't hesitate to show him her love. With him by her side, she could conquer anything. She wasn't a wimpy princess. Well, she *wasn't* a princess at all, but she wasn't wimpy, either.

Her head held high, she stepped forward and made her way to the podium. As she reached it, she took Juan Carlos's outstretched hand and gazed into his eyes. In them, she saw her life, her future. The details were negotiable, but the love, that never wavered. She loved him. She would always love him. Thank God, King Montoro of Alma was a determined man.

Juan Carlos pulled her close and there before the world, bruised her lips in a kiss that left no one doubting their king's commitment. "Juan Carlos," she murmured. "Everyone's watching."

"Are they?"

Cameras clicked like crazy and she had no doubt this epic scene would go viral.

When Juan Carlos broke off the kiss, he nudged her tight to his side to present a united front and turned to the crowd. "Portia is a wonderful, bright, talented woman and in the days and years to come, you will all see in her what I see. I ask only that you welcome her today. Give her the same chance you gave me."

The crowd was silent and Portia's heart plummeted. And then a sole cheer rang out from a man shouting his support. And then another cheer went up and another, in a show of loyalty. And soon, the entire gathering displayed their acceptance as boisterous cheers and booming applause echoed against the palace walls, the citizens of Alma giving the king their allegiance.

They had accepted her.

Portia couldn't keep a wide, teary-eyed smile from spreading across her face. She was grateful for their support, but she was certain that even if the crowd had turned hostile, nothing would have deterred Juan Carlos. He had her back, and that was the best feeling in the world.

The speech over, Portia walked off with Juan Carlos. "I love you, you know," she said, winding her arm around his waist and leaning her head on his shoulder.

"I do know, but I think I'll need to hear you say it about a thousand times. Tonight?"

She nodded. "Tonight." She lifted her lips to his. "Do you think you can make me say it a thousand times?"

He laughed. "Oh, I know I can. Just let me alert the chauffeur we'll be needing the limo soon."

Her eyes went wide. "Juan Carlos, you don't play fair!"

"Sweetheart, I play for keeps. Princess or not, you're a royal temptation that I can't live without."

"So you're keeping me?"

"For as long as you'll have me."

"Forever, then. It's settled."

"Settled," he said, grinning as he picked her up and twirled her around and around.

She floated on air.

And her feet never did touch the ground again.

Epilogue

One month later

Juan Carlos couldn't stop grinning as he held Portia in his arms and danced to the royal orchestra's rendition of "Unforgettable" under hundreds of strung lights and a moonlit sky on the grounds of the newly restored farmhouse. This place that Bella and James would someday call home was where Juan Carlos and Portia had found love, too, and it seemed fitting to have a small intimate exchange of promised vows here in front of their close friends and family. His new bride dressed in satin and ivory lace, with his mother's diamond wedding ring sparkling on her finger, was the most beautiful woman on the planet.

"Are you happy?" he asked, fairly certain his answer was found in the sky-blue gleam in her eyes.

"I don't think I've ever been happier."

"That's how I want to keep it, sweetheart." He pressed her close and kissed her forehead, brushing his lips over her cheeks and nose and finally landing on her sweet mouth.

"I loved our sunset wedding," Portia said. "This is a special place."

Their first dance ended and Juan Carlos swung Portia to a stop in the center of the circle of their guests, who applauded them, their dance and their marriage. Portia's elegant grace, her help in discovering the hidden artworks and her work with local charities had endeared her to the country. Even the doubters had begun to come around as she constantly proved to them that she belonged at his side. It was a good thing, too, because Juan Carlos would rather give up the throne than live without Portia.

His cousins approached. "Welcome to the family, Portia," Rafe said, his very pregnant wife on his arm. "We couldn't be happier for you both."

"It was a lovely ceremony," Emily said.

"Thank you. I've heard all about your special ceremony, as well," Portia offered, glancing at Emily, Rafe, Gabe and Serafia. "I've never attended a double wedding before."

"We wish we would've known you then," Serafia added.

"Might've been a triple wedding, who knows?" Gabe said with a teasing smile.

Juan Carlos found it all amusing. His cousins had met their wives in uncanny ways and now every one of them was married. Rafe had resumed his position as head of Montoro Enterprises and the company was thriving. Good thing, too, because Rafe's father had decided to retire in Alma. After the ceremony he'd been the first to offer his congratulations, giving Portia a kiss on the cheek and wrapping Juan Carlos in a tight embrace. Juan Carlos owed a great deal to the man who had raised him from early childhood.

Gabe, the younger of his male cousins, had finally shed his bad boy ways and settled down with his lifelong friend and love, Serafia.

"I think I just felt something," Bella announced. She took James's hand and placed it on her small rounded belly. "Here, see if you can feel the baby."

James kept his hand there several seconds. "I'm not sure," he said softly, diplomatically. "It's early yet, isn't it, honey?"

"Maybe for you, but I think I felt it." Bella's eyes were two bright beams of light. She was carrying James's child.

James kissed her lips. "I can't wait to feel our baby, too."

Portia slipped her hand in Juan Carlos's and they watched the scene play out. James had one child already and Bella was proving to be a fantastic stepmother to one-year-old Maisey. And now, their family was expanding. Juan Carlos was glad that Bella and James had settled in Alma and James was back playing professional soccer—football as they called it here—and winning games for the home team. Things had been rough there for a while between James and his father, oil tycoon Patrick Rowling. Patrick had picked James's twin brother, Will, to marry Bella. The arranged marriage was an antiquated notion to say the least, and Bella was having none of it. James was the man for her. And then Will had also found love with Catalina Ibarra, his father's maid. The whole thing had sent Patrick into a nosedive but he was finally coming around and softening to the idea that perhaps his sons could make up their own minds about their love life and beyond.

"Now that we're all here together, I have good news to share with all of you," Juan Carlos said. He couldn't help his ever-present smile from intensifying. He had his family's attention now. "I'm told by Alex and the prime minister that Alma has never seen a better year. The country is well on its way to being financially solvent again. Thanks in part to our efforts here, I might add. With the discovery of the lost art treasure, tourism will climb, especially once we put those pieces on public display. We are working to that end. Since the state of Alma is now finally secure once again, a sizable portion of the Montoro fortune has been repatriated. It has been decided that the money will fund a new public school system named for my grandmother Isabella Salazar."

"That's wonderful," Bella said.

Rafe and Gabe slapped him on the back with congratulations.

"If it wasn't for Tia Isabella's determination to see the Montoros return to Alma in her lifetime—and those letters I discovered—none of this would even be possible," Bella said.

It was true. Juan Carlos wouldn't be king, he would never have met Portia and who knew what would have happened among his other family members. "We owe my grandmother quite a bit."

They took a solemn moment to give thanks to Isabella.

And then the orchestra music started up again.

Couples paired off and moved onto the dance floor.

Little Maisey Rowling had woken up from her nap. Wearing pink from head to toe, she was sitting on the front porch playing with the palace kittens alongside Portia's maids in attendance, Jasmine and Maria Ramon.

"I owe those two women a dance," Juan Carlos said to Portia. "If not for them, you may never have come back to Alma. Actually, I owe them much more than that."

"Yes, but first, my love, I have a wedding gift for you. I hope it will match the one you gave me. I cannot wait another second to give it to you."

"Okay," he said, eager to please her. "I'm yours."

She tugged him to the back of the house, to the garden area that was in full bloom, despite the late fall climate. Oh, the miracle of royalty that made all things possible. She sat him down on the white iron bench and then took a seat beside him.

"Juan Carlos," she began, taking his hands and holding them in her lap. "You have given me your love, a new family and a beautiful palace to live in."

"You deserve all those things, sweetheart."

"But there's one thing missing. One thing I want and hope you want, too."

He had no clue where she was going with this. He had everything he wanted. "Have you found another brood of cats to adopt?"

She shook her head and grinned, her eyes beaming with the same glow he'd seen in Bella's. His heart stopped beating. He gathered his thoughts and came to the only conclusion he could.

"You're not?"

She nodded now, bobbing her head up and down rapidly. "I am."

"We're going to have a baby?"

"Yes!"

A glance at her belly gave him no indication. "When?"

"Seven months from now."

Carefully, he pulled her onto his lap. "I'm…I'm…going to be a father."

"Yes, you are."

He curved his hand around her nape and brought his lips close to hers. "You're going to be a mother."

"Yes."

The idea filled him with pride. His Portia would give him a child. It was the best gift in the world. His mouth touched hers reverently and he tasted the sweetness of her lips. "I couldn't be happier, sweetheart."

"I'm glad. Our baby will grow up in a home filled with love. Neither one of us knew our parents for very long. But now, we will have a family of our own. It's quite unexpected…"

"It's all I've ever wanted, Portia. For us to be a family."

"Really?"

He nodded. His throat constricted. His emotions had finally caught up to him today. His life had come full circle—the orphaned boy who would be king, married to his heart's desire, was to have a family all his own now.

There was no better kingdom on earth than for a man to share his life with the woman he loved.

He and Portia were two of a kind.

Almas Iguales.

Equal souls.

* * * * *

DYNASTIES: THE MONTOROS
*One royal family must choose between love and destiny!
Don't miss a single story!*

MINDING HER BOSS'S BUSINESS
by Janice Maynard

CARRYING A KING'S CHILD
by Katherine Garbera

SEDUCED BY THE SPARE HEIR
by Andrea Laurence

THE PRINCESS AND THE PLAYER
by Kat Cantrell

MAID FOR A MAGNATE
by Jules Bennett

A ROYAL TEMPTATION
by Charlene Sands

*If you're on Twitter, tell us what you think of
Harlequin Desire! #harlequindesire.*

MILLS & BOON®
Hardback – October 2015

ROMANCE

Claimed for Makarov's Baby	Sharon Kendrick
An Heir Fit for a King	Abby Green
The Wedding Night Debt	Cathy Williams
Seducing His Enemy's Daughter	Annie West
Reunited for the Billionaire's Legacy	Jennifer Hayward
Hidden in the Sheikh's Harem	Michelle Conder
Resisting the Sicilian Playboy	Amanda Cinelli
The Return of Antonides	Anne McAllister
Soldier, Hero...Husband?	Cara Colter
Falling for Mr December	Kate Hardy
The Baby Who Saved Christmas	Alison Roberts
A Proposal Worth Millions	Sophie Pembroke
The Baby of Their Dreams	Carol Marinelli
Falling for Her Reluctant Sheikh	Amalie Berlin
Hot-Shot Doc, Secret Dad	Lynne Marshall
Father for Her Newborn Baby	Lynne Marshall
His Little Christmas Miracle	Emily Forbes
Safe in the Surgeon's Arms	Molly Evans
Pursued	Tracy Wolff
A Royal Temptation	Charlene Sands

0915 GEN STD HB

MILLS & BOON®
Large Print – October 2015

ROMANCE

The Bride Fonseca Needs	Abby Green
Sheikh's Forbidden Conquest	Chantelle Shaw
Protecting the Desert Heir	Caitlin Crews
Seduced into the Greek's World	Dani Collins
Tempted by Her Billionaire Boss	Jennifer Hayward
Married for the Prince's Convenience	Maya Blake
The Sicilian's Surprise Wife	Tara Pammi
His Unexpected Baby Bombshell	Soraya Lane
Falling for the Bridesmaid	Sophie Pembroke
A Millionaire for Cinderella	Barbara Wallace
From Paradise...to Pregnant!	Kandy Shepherd

HISTORICAL

A Mistress for Major Bartlett	Annie Burrows
The Chaperon's Seduction	Sarah Mallory
Rake Most Likely to Rebel	Bronwyn Scott
Whispers at Court	Blythe Gifford
Summer of the Viking	Michelle Styles

MEDICAL

Just One Night?	Carol Marinelli
Meant-To-Be Family	Marion Lennox
The Soldier She Could Never Forget	Tina Beckett
The Doctor's Redemption	Susan Carlisle
Wanted: Parents for a Baby!	Laura Iding
His Perfect Bride?	Louisa Heaton

MILLS & BOON®

Hardback – November 2015

ROMANCE

A Christmas Vow of Seduction	Maisey Yates
Brazilian's Nine Months' Notice	Susan Stephens
The Sheikh's Christmas Conquest	Sharon Kendrick
Shackled to the Sheikh	Trish Morey
Unwrapping the Castelli Secret	Caitlin Crews
A Marriage Fit for a Sinner	Maya Blake
Larenzo's Christmas Baby	Kate Hewitt
Bought for Her Innocence	Tara Pammi
His Lost-and-Found Bride	Scarlet Wilson
Housekeeper Under the Mistletoe	Cara Colter
Gift-Wrapped in Her Wedding Dress	Kandy Shepherd
The Prince's Christmas Vow	Jennifer Faye
A Touch of Christmas Magic	Scarlet Wilson
Her Christmas Baby Bump	Robin Gianna
Winter Wedding in Vegas	Janice Lynn
One Night Before Christmas	Susan Carlisle
A December to Remember	Sue MacKay
A Father This Christmas?	Louisa Heaton
A Christmas Baby Surprise	Catherine Mann
Courting the Cowboy Boss	Janice Maynard

MILLS & BOON®
Large Print – November 2015

ROMANCE

The Ruthless Greek's Return	Sharon Kendrick
Bound by the Billionaire's Baby	Cathy Williams
Married for Amari's Heir	Maisey Yates
A Taste of Sin	Maggie Cox
Sicilian's Shock Proposal	Carol Marinelli
Vows Made in Secret	Louise Fuller
The Sheikh's Wedding Contract	Andie Brock
A Bride for the Italian Boss	Susan Meier
The Millionaire's True Worth	Rebecca Winters
The Earl's Convenient Wife	Marion Lennox
Vettori's Damsel in Distress	Liz Fielding

HISTORICAL

A Rose for Major Flint	Louise Allen
The Duke's Daring Debutante	Ann Lethbridge
Lord Laughraine's Summer Promise	Elizabeth Beacon
Warrior of Ice	Michelle Willingham
A Wager for the Widow	Elisabeth Hobbes

MEDICAL

Always the Midwife	Alison Roberts
Midwife's Baby Bump	Susanne Hampton
A Kiss to Melt Her Heart	Emily Forbes
Tempted by Her Italian Surgeon	Louisa George
Daring to Date Her Ex	Annie Claydon
The One Man to Heal Her	Meredith Webber

015 GEN STD LP

MILLS & BOON®

Why shop at millsandboon.co.uk?

Each year, thousands of romance readers find their perfect read at millsandboon.co.uk. That's because we're passionate about bringing you the very best romantic fiction. Here are some of the advantages of shopping at www.millsandboon.co.uk:

* **Get new books first**—you'll be able to buy your favourite books one month before they hit the shops

* **Get exclusive discounts**—you'll also be able to buy our specially created monthly collections, with up to 50% off the RRP

* **Find your favourite authors**—latest news, interviews and new releases for all your favourite authors and series on our website, plus ideas for what to try next

* **Join in**—once you've bought your favourite books, don't forget to register with us to rate, review and join in the discussions

Visit **www.millsandboon.co.uk**
for all this and more today!